T0105035

Travel Light

Travel Light

A Sci-Fi romance novel

YVES BALTHAZAR

ARCHWAY
PUBLISHING

Copyright © 2014 Yves Balthazar.

All rights reserved. No part of this book may be used or reproduced by any means, graphic, electronic, or mechanical, including photocopying, recording, taping or by any information storage retrieval system without the written permission of the publisher except in the case of brief quotations embodied in critical articles and reviews.

Archway Publishing books may be ordered through booksellers or by contacting:

Archway Publishing
1663 Liberty Drive
Bloomington, IN 47403
www.archwaypublishing.com
1-(888)-242-5904

Because of the dynamic nature of the Internet, any web addresses or links contained in this book may have changed since publication and may no longer be valid. The views expressed in this work are solely those of the author and do not necessarily reflect the views of the publisher, and the publisher hereby disclaims any responsibility for them.

Any people depicted in stock imagery provided by Thinkstock are models, and such images are being used for illustrative purposes only.
Certain stock imagery © Thinkstock.

ISBN: 978-1-4808-0778-5 (sc)
ISBN: 978-1-4808-0779-2 (e)

Library of Congress Control Number: 2014908806

Printed in the United States of America

Archway Publishing rev. date: 05/08/2014

A Promising Teacher

There was something unique about her beauty, a happy assemblage of features and expression, exotic yet familiar purely and paradoxically by its rarity, and the revelation of which completed the divine inventory of all things beautiful and graceful. His heart had heard nature cry out to heaven to fill that void, and amend that most glaring of oversights. Up to that day, up to the moment that his eyes consumed her, he had not been aware of the nature of the quest, but there she stood, smiling and seeming unaware of her own brilliance.

He was on the verge of saying something trivial and mundane, like "you're so beautiful," but how... and what do you say to a goddess? Besides, he needed to remain calm and lucid, and let his mind and memory absorb that moment. He must have said plenty with his eyes, he must have; he was only human. Then again, she must have heard it all. To her by then, men were like children on Halloween nights, trying to impress her with their cries of "trick or treat," and their tried-hard-but-not-so-original-costumes. Did she care to hear their praises; could she see the cool smiles anymore? Oh, they were all sincere; how could they not be? She could inspire ingredients for the recipe of any compliment. But it was such a surprise to find her in that environment, and an even bigger surprise to discover intelligence in such a beautiful woman. He had once believed that the pretty ones did not feel the need to be bright, and had no urgency to acquire knowledge. He never entertained the thought that they were less endowed with mental abilities, but they were almost invariably found in the most trite of circumstances with the most... well, undeserving of men.

He had always been shy, and the presence of a pretty girl had a way of disconnecting from his mind his ability to verbalize. But, this time – enveloped by her proximity, intoxicated by her scent, drawn into her smile, transported to an unfamiliarly secure state by the power of his wish – he spoke; not of his love, not about the poems that he secretly had been writing for her. He told her that she was a great teacher, and that he had learned more from her than from any other. She simply smiled, a knowing smile that had him walking on air for days until he saw her again.

But he knew. He knew he was deluding himself; she was too beautiful, too bright, and too far from the dream that he should allow himself to dream. He was barely above ground; she was in the stratosphere. No, she was in another world, a world of words, of PhD's, of pedantry, of oak wood desks and secretaries. He was only a freshman, for heaven's sake; less than a footnote, in a few hours, in a day, in a week of a random semester of her rich and busy career. What could he be hoping? Even a wish seemed so unrealistic, so... ethereal! What then? The most he could expect was a zany remembrance after the cure. For in a little while, healing, not requital, will have had been what he required. At least he could still enjoy the consolation of seeing her walk into the doorway in all her splendor, the velvet of her smile gently and remotely brushing the morning boredom off the male students' faces.

From his seat, second on the right side of the U shaped arrangement of tables and chairs, he found it easy to visualize every concealed curve and soft recess of her ravishing anatomy. It was always hard for him to concentrate during the first five minutes of class, so ecstatic was he at the sight of her. No matter how hard he had prepared himself, the rate of his pulse would seemingly triple with every unmistakable sound of her approaching steps on the hard surface of the hallway. The little game that he had started playing recently had helped somewhat. He had been trying to guess the color she would wear, and, as if by some psychic connection, he surprisingly had been right more often then not. Many times, he successfully matched the same color with his shirt.

Once the awkward moment had passed, he was able to apply himself to his favorite pastime in class: impress her with his mind, dazzle her with his quick wit, and amuse her with his jocularity. He wanted her to know that she was his prime focus; she certainly would not mistake his demeanor for brashness. Sure, she had seen it many times before: another victim of her charm begging to be noticed; but at least this one was not some male bimbo, or some jock trying to impress her with his sinew. He was always prepared; he had studied. Something else was different about him; he was older. She had developed a technique for dealing with those lovesick puppies, but this one was going to require a new course of action. For the others, it was simple; she would pair them up in study or presentation groups with young women closer to their age and interests, and voila! Nature would do its thing.

She could tell early on that the same strategy was not going to work with Lance. She knew that he had made up his mind about her, as if it were a simple matter of time before she sent a telepathic message saying, "*Yes, I'm ready to be yours.*" She had always tried to give equal attention to all her students. Lately, however, she had been looking his way more. She had been more attentive to his inquiries, and more receptive to his answers. At first realization of what was for her a most serious transgression, she panicked; not her, she was stronger than that! She had heard of such things taking place, especially with male teachers; female teachers are judged by a harsher scale. After a while, she began to look upon it as a manageable distraction; she had done nothing to encourage it! She had a long time ago come to terms with her being beautiful. More than that, she was secure in the knowledge that her intelligence had carried her through. Perhaps, it was time for her to drop that obtrusive scale of moral fortitude and allow herself to fly unencumbered. Didn't she deserve a sin or two? She thought of joining in that flirtatious dance with him; she thought him mature enough to handle it. After all, he started it! But wait… could she handle it?

As she took her position behind the large Formica table at the top of the 'U', Lance began his now familiar chant,

"Please, look at me and smile. Please, look at…"

"Lance," shouted a chorus of voices.

He turned to the loudest and unfamiliar one to his left.

"I'm sorry," he mumbled embarrassingly, thinking that he had unwillingly vocalized his plea.

"Miss King wants to know… your presentation… Are you ready?" said professor Rhoades, the man in the seat to his left.

"I… er, yes," he muttered.

He shuffled some paper and cards in front of him, took a brief survey of the class, and offered her a smile that was brushed off with an impatient nod, to the amusement of his classmates.

"My composition is titled *Prisms*," he began.

He spoke for the next twenty-five minutes without a pause. He spoke as if he were an actor doing his best to move an audience to fear. His voice rose, fell, cracked, and then settled. He sat, he stood, he leaned, he trotted, he leaped, and he mimed, and painted pictures with every part of his body. Then as suddenly as he had begun, he stopped, appearing spent and pallid. He managed an unfocussed smile in her direction before falling back in his seat with a "Thank you."

Professor Rhoades was the first to break the thick and paralyzing silence that had fallen upon the room, followed by Miss King whose applause hastened to match professor Rhoades's rhythm. Five long seconds had passed before Marilyn's exuberant 'yes' started a cascade of handclaps and cheers of every sort from an audience more inclined to deriding during and after Lance's often controversial overtures. He received a tap on the back from professor Rhoades, and a loud kiss from Marilyn. Miss King simply said "great job," but with a smile that time – one of her prettiest! How could he know how proud she felt at that moment? No one could guess the struggle she was about to face, or the choice she will have had to make.

Lance tried his best to keep his attention on a half dozen more presentations from the others while he ruminated the questions he planned to ask her at the end of the session. He needed to satisfy the hunger for being closer to her voluptuousness, just for a moment, just long enough to cast another week's worth of dreams. Meanwhile Marilyn was inching ever closer, her left arm stroking his right, her eyes begging for his attention. She had been his defender against the wild bunch of back-row-rabble-rousers that had tried to make him their whipping boy. She knew how to deal with that kind; she had been one of them not long ago. Someone like Lance would have been her victim, but in her new frame of mind, she saw in him a symbol of redemption for herself. In addition, he was a different kind of bookworm; he looked fine and he knew how to stand up for himself. She was going to bring into winning him that same sense of purpose that she had carried over from the hood and into this new environment.

"Lance," called Marilyn with the soft voice that she used only for him and no one else, "Can you hurry up? I wanna go eat something."

He turned to look at her for the first time since the start of the session. Ah! She was pretty, especially with a smile, and without the tough expression.

"Sorry babe," he said, trying to sound casual, "I have to talk to Miss King about that final paper. I'm having some problems..."

She turned quickly without saying another word and headed toward the door. He stealthily watched her walk away; her style and grace could have made a professional model jealous. He had always found her attractive, but in this new environment, and with the semester nearly over, he was discovering her anew. She had the kind of figure that had never failed to enrapture him – shoulders that extruded from the base of the neck nearly horizontally, ending in tight smooth curves, a torso with the right size and shape of adornments, and the daintiest little waist to veer one's attention toward curvier regions and render the senses captive of susceptibilities primal and libidinous. When she walked, she unleashed a graceful symphony of sways, spins, twists, heaves, swings, bounces, and slides; all to an effortless cadence that made him question her alleged past allegiance to the streets.

Professor Rhoades had engaged Miss King in conversation right after her first good bye to the class. He was doing most of the talking. Lance could not make out the words, or the matter being discussed. He had packed and unpacked his bag a couple of times, awaiting his chance to be alone with Miss. King. He was running the risk of being conspicuous or worst appearing inquisitive. Finally, he decided to leave. Just then, he heard Miss King calling,

"Lance, have you met professor Rhoades? Professor Rhoades is a faculty member of our university; he is the head of the psychology department. He was here to observe; I told the class last week. He was quite impressed with your presentation."

"Very impressive" added professor Rhoades, "I hope to have you in my class next semester. I teach Intro…"

"I hope to be Sir, thank you. Thanks a lot!" interrupted Lance. He turned to collect his bag and rushed out, his hunger unsatisfied.

Slides

I t was a small room, cluttered with every size and shape of appliances. One could tell judging by the dust and the way things were stored pell-mell that they had not been used or touched in a while. Most of them looked like plain metal boxes fitted with round or square glass windows. The larger ones displayed rows of small transparent disks arranged according to colors and sizes. The walls were bare except for the foot square plaque above the big console that seemed to offer instructions in a foreign language on operational procedure. The man approached as if to read it, and then turned to face the round shaped window. Protruding out of that window was a fifteen-foot long cylinder, a foot in diameter, which appeared to be pointed to the stars. There were no apparent connections, no wiring or other visible links between those machines and the telescope at the porthole. He returned to the large console and searched the rear for a switch. With hardly an audible click, the room became a Christmas display. All the little discs, squares, and LED lights of every color came on. It should have been uncomfortable and disorientating to anyone, but he seemed quite at ease. He walked up to the telescope-like apparatus, examined its various controls and dials, and located an eyepiece into which he peered for a few seconds. After some readjustments, he found his target. He recorded his observations, and then returned to the main console. He was about to input some additional instructions when what sounded like an army busted into the building, and in a second was at the door demanding immediate entry.

He was running harder than he had ever run before. He had never been a good or fast runner, but he felt as if he were flying. Desperation can inspire great feats, and at that moment, he desperately needed to get away from his pursuers. He did not feel his feet making contact with the ground. He did not feel the wind rushing past his face. He could not remember – if he had time to ponder – how he had escaped from that room. Buildings, whole blocks whisked by in his periphery. Occasionally, a landmark or a hunch influenced a right or left turn. A string of awnings ran uninterrupted to the end of a darkened block, giving him the impression of running on the inside of a tunnel. Up ahead, on the left segment of a cross street, he spotted a row of doors equally spaced and resembling those of a storage facility. The roof above those doors laid a mere six feet above street level. At the intersection, he crossed diagonally toward the peculiar structure to find that he had to run down five or six steps to the block-long path along which the doors stood. He inexplicably found the only unlocked room, slid in, and in less than a minute, he was feeling calm and comfortable. Against the back wall, he discovered a small bed, and on the bed what appeared to be the shape of a man sleeping undisturbed. He sat motionless for a short while, and then turned to face the wall. He studied the grooves and patterns, he ran his fingers inside the vertical crinkles, tapped with his knuckles, and then looked down at a point where the wall met the floor, and up to a point where it touched the ceiling. He resolved that everything was as it should be; that it was not a dream. It certainly was a strange night; so much happened so quickly. For now, he was too exhausted to make sense of everything; he brought his attention back to the bed and decided to go to sleep.

He had had strange experiences in the past when he had been in the gray areas between sleeping and waking states. Many times, the lack of cogitative separation between the two had left him to wonder what was real. It was not the first time that he had felt the need to substantiate his state of consciousness. He could clearly recall the night he awakened to find himself spinning horizontally inches above the bed. He became conscious in mid turn, and when he stopped, he was facing the opposite wall. He was on his right side, a fraction of a second before he had been on his left. He was now face to face with a thing, a being; an entity barely taller than the bed was high. The troll-like figure took off toward the nearest corner as soon as it realized that he was conscious. In a flash, it ducked behind a nightstand. *"I have to do something,"* he thought; this time there will be no question as to whether or not he was awake. He got on his feet from his frozen sitting position and gave chase, but there was nothing *stirring* or otherwise, *not even a mouse.* The windows were still closed, and there was no sound of anyone leaving the apartment. He spent the remainder of the night wondering why he had awoken in that fashion; turning as he did in mid air while he was still unconscious. It was as if he were aware of that presence even then.

His first recollection of something surreal – although at the time he would not have been able to qualify it as such – went back to his childhood. He was eight years old and in bed with a high fever. He awakened to find himself floating up toward a bright sphere, which he thought was the sun. He felt no heat, only a sense of wellness and peace. His parents tried to assure him that he had been dreaming, and that the fever must have caused him to hallucinate. They did not explain why he got out of bed right after the 'dream,' feeling well and cheerful. The fact that the memory of it never wane was also significant. On another occasion, he saw himself being guided into his fourth-floor bedroom window by a child-like entity while lying on a floating gurney. He then was gently placed on his bed where he observed the curtains blowing out of the window as they had been at his entrance.

The *piece de resistance* was the incident at the pier. It was a beautiful summer afternoon when boys go out looking for adventure and trouble. There they were on the pier, one hundred feet from land, looking down at the water. His friend, somewhat of a bully, had talked him into going out to the docks when they should have been at a boys-scout meeting. He always listened with envy to the stories of the other boys who were good swimmers and divers. He had never learned to swim; home life was strict, school and church were held as the only valid reasons to be away from its shelter. As he stood there in awe of the great expense of blue wetness, a voice behind him ordered,

"Jump."

He turned to find his companion's contorted face six inches from his,

"Jump or I'll throw you in," the bully repeated with cold calm, but firmly.

"But... but you know I can't swim, I'll..."

"You're not going back until you dive in," threatened the hulk.

He knew he could not go past the bigger boy to the safety of firm land. His supplications had no effect on the young hood's malignant soul. He tried negotiating,

"O.k., what if I climb down... I'll be in the water; same thing, right?

The oaf thought for a second.

"Go ahead, hurry up," he ordered.

He climbed down a diagonal brace into the water and started dog pedaling furiously. He stayed afloat for a few seconds, but just when he was beginning to gain some confidence, he started to sink. The proverbial life flashing before one's eyes became all too real. He saw every bit of his fourteen years between the first and second gulp of salt water. Then he heard himself think, *"oh, my mother's gonna kill me,"* which might have quickened his resignation to just let go if it were not for those feet which appeared out of nowhere, kicking as they went up toward the surface. He reached for them and held on with all his might. The funny thing was, as he remembered, the owner of those feet did not miss a stroke or panic as he continued his effortless ascent. He was deposited exactly at the point where he had gotten into the water. As he held on to the beam, coughing, regurgitating, and gasping for air, he looked all around for his rescuer, but there wasn't anyone nearby, in or out of the water, or under the surface as far as he was able to tell. The young hood was still standing up on the pier where he had left him, dry and ostensibly disappointed. He, too, had seen no one else.

There had been so many encounters, so many unexplained and unexplainable happenings in his life that he could not as hard as he tried relegate them all to the realm of dreams, optical illusions, or hallucinations. Lately, he had been having those dreams; dreams of future events, of places that he had not seen before, and of people that he had never met, and he had seen those events unfold, and met those individuals. He had seen himself move to a new place about which he had dreamt. He had saved himself from danger by taking the prescribed course of action, predicted outcomes of relationships, and been shown the right decisions, and more. He often asked himself whether he was being looked after by a benevolent power from above; whether he had been enrolled in God's Witness Protection Program. He had always found that the world was divided into two camps as far as he was concerned, those who loved and admired him intensely, and those who likewise, and for reasons he could never understand, arbor resentment toward him. He always, however, embraced each morning with the same buoyant energy and optimism, and entered every portal with equal curiosity and expectancy, regardless of the previous day's disappointments.

The Helicopter Flight

"Hello, who is this?"

"Don't say another word; go out to your living room," said the voice on the phone.

"I'm sorry, I cannot hear you, there's this damned helicopter taking off. Speak louder," screamed Rhoades, as he picked up his bag and started toward the front door.

"Just keep walking," said the voice at the other end.

"Jesus Christ, man! What are you... trying to give me a heart attack? Can't you just knock on the door and wait like everyone else? How did you get in here anyway? Never mind, I'm going to be late, can you drive me? I'll get a ride back tonight."

"Ok! Still the same Phil. Calm down, one question at the time;" said the intruder, "first one first... You know your door is always open for me, right. Of course, I'll give you a ride, but I'm not driving, that was my helicopter taking off; well, not mine, the University's. Just a minute, I'll call it back. Who's giving you a ride back? Got a date, huh?"

The man, whom Rhoades recognized as his old friend, Taggart, pulled a black stick from his breast pocket, the size of a tongue depressor, and spoke in some letters and digits. He then stood up and came toward Rhoades who was still at the spot where he had dropped his cup of tea, mouth open and shaking his head in amused disbelief.

"What is that thing? What are you today, James Bond, Arnold Schwarzenegger, Tom Cruise?" he asked.

"What's today, Friday? The name is Jones, Indiana Jones," Taggart giggled as he put his arms around Phil's shoulders and nudged him toward the front door. He pointed to the horizon at the vague shape of an approaching helicopter.

"Seriously, what are you? What is it that you really do?" Phil asked.

"We're in the same business, Phil, shaping young minds. Occasionally, one of those young minds has something to reveal to us. Something that might change the world, indeed save it. You know what I'm saying, Phil?"

"Wait a minute, let me understand this; we have this conversation last night, and I casually tell you about this young man and his dreams and experiences. So, at first light this morning, you commandeer the first helicopter you can find, pilot included I might add, from the university's parking lot I guess, break and enter my house, and now we're off on some adventure to save the world. Is that about right?"

"For the sake of argument, yes!"

"Jesus! I feel like Albert Brooks in the 'In-laws,' and I'm being kidnap by fake CIA man, Michael Douglas."

"Aaaahhh... excuse me, Mr. Rhoades; sorry, I'm... er, really confused, but aren't you the impulsive, adventurous one? I... er..." rambled Taggart in a bad Lt. Colombo impersonation.

"Who's that? Hum... Listen, I'm a responsible adult now; I try to act like one. Besides, what does this have to do with archaeology? That is your field now, isn't it? Wait, don't answer yet, I'll give you time to think. I want this to make sense when I tell Tina."

The flight was silent. Occasionally, each in turn took glancing look at the other, smiling, until finally Phil gently elbowed Taggart and said,

"It's always good to see you, you lunatic."

"Good to see you, maniac," Taggart elbowed back, "how long has it been this time, a year, two? You should really consider coming to Georgetown. I can really use someone like you. With your analytical, theoretical mind, and your knowledge of physics, you'd be a perfect collaborator in this, and other projects of ours. Besides, things are getting tight up there, Phil. You know how it is, our budget is shrinking; we have to do more with less. With you, we will be able to satisfy two, three needs at once. Not just on this project…"

"You don't waste any time at all with your sales pitch. I hope it's still good to see me as well."

"What is this project you're working on? Dream analysis?" Taggart continued, ignoring Phil's comment.

"See, that's the problem, you're too self-absorbed. I hate to tell you, but I'm sure you know that about yourself, don't you?"

"Come on," Taggart continued, undeterred, "What's keeping you here? We both know you can do better. Listen, you help me with this and I'll make sure you get a grant for any study you want to embark on"

"Any study, huh? I did not know you had that much power up there."

"Not me, it's what we can give them, Phil. They really want this thing, and I know we can deliver. We always had great synergy; together we could always come up with the answer to any question, solve any puzzle; remember?"

"Sounds like some kind of holy grail," mugs Phil.

"Well, this can be big, my friend, very big!"

Phil's smile betrayed the coming of a witty remark, but instead he offered,

"If you can wait a year, I'll be able to make a decision then."

"A year, a year," Taggart exploded in laugher, "you hope that's how long it'll take to convince her. There's a dream you need to analyze! Wake up and smell the nail polish, my friend. She's been dragging you by the nose; well, you want her to do that. It's a way for you stay close to her, isn't it; better that then nothing, huh?"

"What are you talking about? Are we still on the same subject?"

"What are you talking about," mimicked Taggart, "Tina; Tina is what this is all about. I've just realized, I've been going at this all wrong. She should have been my initial target; convince her to come to Washington and you'll come running."

"Listen, you're way out of line now. You say something like that to piss me off, don't you? What am I supposed to do now? Prove to you that you're wrong? Drop everything and follow you to Washington? By the way, it wasn't too long ago that she'd snap her fingers and you'd jump like a puppy. Lucky for you she's not the type..."

"Been there, done that, and that may be why I can see what is happening to you, bro."

"No, no, it's something else. I thing you're jealous, Tag. With all your talk of success and independence, you envy me; you envy my friendship with Tina; our closeness. You didn't leave because you cared less; no, you loved her more, more than I probably did. You're right, I'm here because of her; she is a friend, and we all need to have friends around. If I go to Washington, it'll be because you asked me to, won't it; I'll know that I'll have a friend there as well, won't I."

"Who?" mocked Taggart with a puzzled look, and feeling that it was time to diffuse the tension that was starting to build; Tina had never been an easy subject to discuss between them.

"Oh, you mean me." He added, "Of course, Phil, you would come because I ask you, sure. It would be strictly platonic though; and don't worry, I don't wear nail polish. Oh, by the way, you have a little red smudge by the left nostril there; been around Tina recently?"

Taggart reached for Phil's nose; Phil quickly pulled his head back. Both man laughed copiously. Just then, the pilot turned to announce that they had reached their destination. A magnificent assortment of edifices in customary gothic and medieval attire came into view. In the middle of it all, a gorgeous expense of green grass, contoured by trees in varying degrees of autumnal trappings, basked in supple glory in the morning sunlight; it will be their landing pad. Green ripples ran furiously for cover in every direction as they approached. The trees showed their objection to the big metallic dragonfly disturbing the serenity of that tranquil setting by waving their branches angrily. As the flying machine began to land, a big burly security officer emerged from the shadows, screaming and signing orders to abort. The pilot took his time setting the helicopter down, then jumped out, and slowly lit a big cigar. He walked toward the uniformed man, meeting him half way, and showed him what appeared to be a badge as they exchanged words. The big man froze, then bowed, smiled, and generally acted as if he had just met the queen of England. He raised both hands and wiped the air in front of him, as if erasing his very presence. He then swiftly retreated, appearing less imposing with every backward step toward the security of the shades. Once the other two men had exited and gotten to a safe distance, the helicopter took off as irreverently as it had landed, leaving two abhorrent parallel impressions in the beautiful organic carpet.

The men reached professor Rhoades' office in good humor. It had been a brisk walk from their impromptu landing, and they were thirsty for coffee. A short trek to the cafeteria was in order. As they sat at a table near the window to enjoy, Taggart inquired,

"When do I get to meet the young man?"

"If I knew you were coming, I would have made sure he slept in my office last night." Phil joked, "listen, I want to talk to him myself, Tag, but today is Friday; we'll have all day. Tina called him last night; she'll bring him over as soon as he's here, which can be any minute now."

Professor Rhoades then checked his watch, leaned back, and smiled.

"Life is short; stop and smell the coffee," he added, looking out at the splendid autumn scene outside; he then took a long, noisy sip.

Such a Beautiful King

The guard standing outside the security booth was taken aback by the unabridged smile and the clear and audible "good morning" he received from Lance.

"Must be the weather," he thought, *"should get ready for all the small talk today."*

Lance had always considered himself a happy and affable person, but too often, someone looked at him and encouraged him to "smile," or advised, "Don't be so serious," or inquired, "What are you so mad about?" That morning, there was no doubt as to the nature of his mood; he was beaming. He was going to see her! He was going to have her all to himself; well, at least her company. Perhaps he will have the courage to tell her, perhaps...

"Hi Lance, you are early. How are you feeling this morning?" said Miss King as she opened the door.

"I'm feeling great, such a beautiful day!" he replied as he considered a place to sit, where the light would compliment his features. Although he had always been told that he was a handsome young man, he often felt the necessity to optimize the opposite sex perception of him. He had long discovered that light could be a useful ally. Miss King seemed even prettier that morning; more feminine. While the dress she wore was unassumingly casual and devoid of any hint of sexual intent, the slightest shift of her body betrayed that sublime physique underneath.

"I'm glad you could come," she smiled as she took a seat at the other end of the sofa; "I have been raving to everyone about your writing. We seem to have similar interests. I'd like to talk about one topic in particular. First, tell me, are those dreams real? What I mean is have you really had those dreams that you mentioned in your presentation?"

"Yes, I have," Lance exhaled; "and you were as beautiful as you are now."

"Excuse me?" she frowned.

"I am sorry... I mean... it's just that I have been practicing telling you... I know it's not, but... I am a little nervous; would you please repeat the question?"

"No need to be nervous, Lance. I'll tell you what; I insist you tell me what you have in mind. Take your time and speak in full sentences. I know you can; okay?"

She reached out and gently tapped his shoulder. Lance giggled silently, then began,

"Two nights ago, I dreamed we were sitting in this very office; I've never been here before, right? You were trying to tell or warn me about something, but all I could think was how beautiful you were; just as I was doing when you started to speak a moment ago."

"Well! Thank you, Lance," smiled Miss King, "you just clarified something for me; I'll tell you one of these days. You are a wonderful young man; most women would give anything to be with you. With me, there's a matter of impropriety, you understand. I really envy all those young ladies out there."

"Well, I will not be a student forever," Lance said wistfully.

"That's true... Now, you remember that on Wednesday, professor Rhoades was here to observe the class. We have been discussing you since. He is conducting a research and he thinks you can be of help.

After hearing your presentation, he has been calling me incessantly. He asked me to speak to you about joining his team on a project. If you agree, we will go see him and he will fill you in on the details. What do you think?"

"What's the nature of the project?"

"It has to do with dream analysis. This is all that I am able to tell you. I thought you might learn something about yourself as well."

The phone rang as Lance was about to speak.

"Tina King's office," she answered, "Oh! you're already here. I thought you would still be crawling on the parkway somewhere... oh, really! Helicopter! Moving up in the world, aren't we... just say when, we've been sitting here chatting, Lance and I... O.K. we'll meet you there. Bye!"

"That was Phil... professor Rhoades. We are going to meet him in his office. Oh, I'm sorry, is it ok? The phone rang before you could give me an answer."

"Definitely yes! Anything for you, Miss King," smiled Lance, "you're going to stay with us for a while, are you?"

"Are you flirting with me, Lance? You don't want to make Marilyn angry, do you?"

"Aaah, we're just friends; that's all."

"Does she know that? She is quite a pretty girl, more your type. Ok... er, are you ready to go see professor Rhoades? It'll simply be an introductory meeting; he'll tell you what you need to know."

As they walked the four-block distance to professor Rhoades' office, Lance fantasized a leisurely promenade in the park with his most lovely conquest. As usual, Miss. King drew everyone's attention, students and faculty personnel alike; male and female. Lance could not be prouder; he took every opportunity to make her laugh and smile, and make the occasion seem less formal and more personal. It must have worked because people, some of whom normally would not have acknowledged him if he had been floating in mid air, were stopping to greet him with "alright, Lance," and "what's happening, man," or "call me, dude;" others raised the victory sign followed by a wink. After a while, Miss King turned to Lance and remarked,

"Aren't you the popular one."

"Oh... they're just happy for me."

"Happy, why?"

"Oh, nothing."

"OK then," she snapped as she walked away from him, pouting.

He rushed to catch up with her; they laughed like two teenagers on a date. By then, they had reached their destination. They entered Professor Rhoades' office to find him shaking his head and displaying an exaggerated expression of admiration. He had seen them cross the street from his window; he had seen her in that dress, her body slithering through the gentle gusts of the breeze.

"Lord," he exclaimed, eyeing her up and down, "haven't you created enough commotion on this campus. If it's for my benefit, I assure you I'm grateful and flattered; if it's not, then I must tell you summer is long gone, you know. Give these young men a break, and the young ladies as well; they must find it hard to compete with Venus incarnated."

"I don't care what the season is; you have been outside, it's practically summer. Besides, Lance thinks I look great, right Lance?"

"Don't embarrassed the poor guy; he probably was just being polite," Phil interceded.

He shook Lance's hand and directed him to a spot on a couch.

"That would really hurt. Is that true Lance, you were just being polite? I believed you," Tina whined.

"Talk about hurt, Guess who is here," professor Rhoades posed.

"I don't know... Sigmund Freud looking for compensation?" Tina joked.

"No, not as smart, and definitely more neurotic."

"I heard that!" declared a muffled voice.

Taggart suddenly emerged from the lavatory; he stopped in the doorway, looking insulted.

"Who said that?" he demanded, "I'll be on 'Are You Smarter than a Fifth Grader' next week, and I'll show you all."

Everybody, including Lance, exploded in laughter. Phil almost choked on his coffee; Tina jumped back to avoid being sprayed and almost landed on Lance's lap.

"Tag!" screamed Tina, "what are you doing here?"

"Ah! Mrs. Rhoades, you are a picture... just a picture. So, he finally got you, huh, this sneaky so and so; turn my back for a couple of years...," said Taggart as he pulled Tina up for a kiss and a hug.

"No, still Miss King I'm afraid. I told you, you two have to fight it out, and the winner may ask my father for my hand in marriage."

"Oh, no! Not that, not that father of yours; I just as well concede. Who is this young man? Tina, are you going younger now? Well, good for you! You know what they say."

"What do they say?" Asked Phil who was still busy swabbing the large coffee stain on his knee.

"I don't know; I'm sure they say something, something like, 'once you go young, you'll always have a song,' yeah," replied Taggart. "Been singing a lot, T.?" then turning toward Lance. "Make sure you do the right thing, young man; I mean, if something unexpected should, you know... develop, her father is a gun collector..."

"And a gun abuser," added Phil. "He should know. Remember that evening; he caught you throwing pebbles at her window. You would have thought WW3 had started."

"He was protecting his little girl from ruffians in the neighborhood, like you two." interrupted Tina, "Oh, you know he wasn't really shooting at you. You guys cannot scare Lance, he is fearless; besides, I'll make sure to go in first and hide all the bullets."

Phil and Taggart turned to each other and uttered a simultaneous "Ooooooh."

"Stop it, you two. Lance, we are just kidding around. Lance is here to meet with you, professor Rhoades."

"Now, behave professor Taggart, Miss King is here," Phil said, pointing to Tina."

"That's O.K; I'm in no hurry," Lance interjected, "I'm enjoying this; I never knew that you, professors, had a sense of humor," he then added, "and I cannot wait to meet the parents, guns and all."

After yet another explosion of laughter had subsided, Taggart, affecting a grave expression, asked,

"We have a sense of humor? We'll thank you to guard it with your life, brave Sir Lancelot; it is against our manifesto. There would be consequences if the Queen should uncover this most forbidden trait in any of her subjects."

Everybody, trembling voices in unison,

"Ooooooooooooh!"

Of course, professor Taggart was alluding to the university's president, Dr. Alana Westbrook, never one to be caught smiling, and too ardent an enforcer of regulations and protocol. Professor Rhoades pulled his chair to a spot where he could face everyone, and suddenly looked solemn.

"Lance, the reason that I am interested in you working with us on our project is that you are the ideal subject for something that requires the attributes that I have come to believe you possess. You are intelligent, sensitive, diligent, and you have this innate ability to dissociate yourself from a personal experience and come up with a rational analysis. In other words, you can be objective. Normally, it is not something that I require of a subject, but in this case, you will be more than a subject; you will be a partner, a collaborator, if you will.

We are not your conventional Dream Research Team. Although some of the methodologies we use come from Dream Research, we depart from it in several key objectives. We are not trying to uncover the mechanism of dreams, or better understand how the brain activates the dream process and so on. There are many other scientists working on those projects, and great advances have been made. Where our research differs is in the 'why' and the 'what else.' In other words, why are dreams necessary? What is the role of dreams in the workings of the human psyche? In addition, what else can we discover about dreams, for the purpose of therapy, both physically and psychologically? A less vital but as desirable an objective will be to ascertain whether dreams can be voluntarily initiated or induced. In the pursuit of these goals, there no doubt will be some ancillary breakthroughs, as happen in many scientific investigations. Actually, you and a soon-to-be-member of our team have inspired some ideas to be explored.

We use a number of different schemes. You will be asked to prepare a brief but intimate biography, the purpose of which will be to help us context your dreams. You will fill out a pertinent questionnaire. You will be asked to keep a journal of your dreams. Whenever necessary, we make use of hypnosis and biofeedback. Once or twice a week, you will be asked to stay overnight in our lab so we can monitor your sleep, and dream pattern. To that end, I have develop a monitoring device that works much like an EEG machine, only with the ability to transfigure brain waves into a kind of language we can more readily decipher.

You will seldom be in contact with other subjects, except, as I mentioned before, one new member with whom we believe you are compatible for a specific undertaking. We may be able to leave this campus to take advantage of more advanced facilities with state of the art, innovative equipment. Our friend, professor Schaffhausen, will make one such facility available to us. Perhaps once or twice within the next month, we will travel to Georgetown University to impose on the good professor. Of course, there is monetary compensation and stipend; we will discuss that confidentially. Anything you'd like to add professor... hum, Taggart."

"All right, I'll let it go this time; next time you'll be *rhoades kill*, professor Rhoades," quipped Taggart, whose last name, Schaffhausen, had always been a subject of jokes and phallic innuendos. Since Taggart sounds like a last name, people who came to know him after high school assumed that it was his actual surname; he seldom bothered to rectify their misapprehension.

"It's OK to call me Taggart," he continued, "I am a psychologist and an archeologist at Georgetown University. We recently discovered a very old but well preserved tablet outside of Jerusalem. It was easy to establish that it was not indigenous of that region. We since have had well known people from various disciplines, some of whom you've heard of, working at determining what it was, where it came from, how old it might be, and so on. All they have been able to tell us thus far is that it is not from any culture with which we are familiar. Our imaging expert is confident that the thing is comprised of a number of tablets fused together by some inscrutable method. The characters, although simple, do not lend themselves to translation by the same techniques that have been used with other ancient writings. Furthermore, carbon dating has been useless in approximating its age, because its content of carbon-14 exceeds by a factor of millions what is realistically acceptable. In short, it remains a mystery. Yours truly, and anyone involved in solving this mystery will become famous, and rich perhaps if you're interested in that sort of thing.

Now, I am going to tell you what your role in all this would be. It is quite significant, and it fits perfectly into your agenda. A few days ago, I received a call from someone who claimed to be able to solve our problem, or a least knew someone who knew someone... We are desperate for a breakthrough, something and anything; besides what would it hurt? I agreed to see him for five or ten minutes; less if he didn't impress me right away. His first words to me were, "he travels to the light; his dreams hold the key." He then proceeded to tell me that he knew what I had, and described the tablet in details. When I told him I did not know what his little charade meant, he told me to wait and that I would know quite soon, and when I do, he will as well. I figured he was some weirdo who has read about our discovery, or that someone from our team had a loose tongue, and I dismissed the whole incident; until last night.

Last night, I got a call from my good friend Phil who, as we often do with one another, was updating me on his project. He happened to mention something that made me sit up at attention on my sofa. He was relating a dream from someone he had just met. The more he spoke, the more exited I became; that's it, I screamed inside my head, that's what he meant, that dear spook. Five minutes later, the phone rang again; I recognized his gravely voice. 'Mr. Spock,' I said, and before I could say another word, he informed me that I'm going on a trip, I should have my bag packed and be ready to leave by 6 am; I'm going to see professor Rhoades. I was flabbergasted, but he assured me that soon I would understand, he also told me that he liked the 'Mr. Spock' moniker, and that from now on, he is Mr. Spock. I did not tell him that I was thinking 'Spook' when I said 'Spock.' Are you starting to see the connection, Phil, Tina?"

Neither Phil nor Tina was ready to answer Taggart's question; they raised their shoulders in a vague expression of non-commitment. Taggart appeared confused by their silence; he did not realize that Lance had not been informed about him, and that they feared that Lance would not like the idea of how much they already seemed to have engaged him.

"He is a tall, skinny, pasty-pale man, is he?" Lance blurted out, breaking the embarrassing silence.

"I don't know!" Taggart answered, "Do you know him? I don't know his real name."

"I don't like him, I would not trust him if I were you." Lance advised.

"Is there something I should know?" Taggart asked, addressing the whole room. "OK Phil, what's going on?"

"I think we owe Lance an apology, and you an explanation," Phil said. "Miss King has known for some time that Lance is a gifted young man, but has kept it to herself. She has told me that he is his prize student, and that having him in her class makes teaching more interesting and more challenging, because of his zest for learning, his complete involvement, and his intelligence. However, until last week, I knew nothing of his gift of premonition, astral projection; his ability to 'see' in his dream and god knows what else we may discover together. Forgive my enthusiasm, Lance, for having shared with professor Taggart what I have learned from your presentation and from Miss King, but in our business someone with your abilities does not happen every day. I assume that professor Taggart's narration brought up memories of something or someone you saw in a dream didn't it?"

"Yes, it did. In a dream, you know instinctively whether someone is good or bad, a positive or a negative entity, everybody is naked so to speak. Until professor Taggart tells us more about this man, we cannot take a chance. I've been wrong by ignoring warnings, and it has cost. I cannot tell you how I know, but this thing you found can be dangerous in the wrong hands, very dangerous."

"Accept my apology as well, Lance," Miss king pitched in, "my belief in the paranormal has brought me some grief, and perhaps I wanted to shield you from ridicule. But you were so passionate in your writings about your experiences that I was swept up in the excitement of reading your papers; I could not help sharing it. You see, the three of us grew up together; we know everything about each other, there is a built-in trust in our friendships…"

"It's OK, I don't care who knows. In fact, I'm flattered that smart, intellectual people like you take interest in me and what you think I can do. Just be careful, professor Taggart."

"I promise to be, Lance. Professor Rhoades, do you think we might have a lab session today? I return to Washington tonight."

"It's up to Lance; we have not planned to have one."

"I'll tell you what, professor Taggart," Lance said, "find out what you can from Mr. Spock; that will determine how we proceed with this. If you can delay your departure, I'll come back tonight for a session. I hope I'm not sounding presumptuous, but we need to be careful."

As they left professor Rhoades' office, the mood was sober. Taggart's revelation, along with Lance's admonition had changed their perception of what to come; from one of scientific adventure to that of a crucial mission wrought with suspense and intrigue.

The Sleepover

"Lance, wait-up!" yelled out the voice.

Lance turned to see Marilyn running toward him in the parking lot. She gave him a spirited kiss and a long hug.

"I haven't seen you in two days; don't you return calls anymore?" she chastised.

"Didn't I speak to you yesterday?" Lance protested.

"No, that was Wednesday, big dummy. You're coming or leaving?"

"Coming."

"At this time? The library is closing. Today is Friday you know, it's our library day; where were you?"

"I had a meeting with professor Rhoades, he has this research thing and he asked me to be a subject."

"Really... Everybody's talking about how they saw you and Miss King walking around campus this morning, laughing and having a good time. I always knew you had a thing for her..."

"She was taking me to professor Rhoades' office. Come on, are you..."

"I am nothing! I just don't wanna see you get hurt. I can tell you're a very sensitive guy, that's nice, and that's what I like about you, but she's up there with the bigs; she's got ambition and you can't blame her for that, but I don't wanna see you get played. I'm just looking out for my friend, ok?"

Lance wanted to tell her that she was jealous and perhaps getting too possessive; he knew that more than friendship motivated her concern, but he being that blunt would have crushed her. He valued their relationship as it was, but he was certain that she expected more, and that she would not tolerate sharing even a small slice of him with someone else. What a challenge!

"Tell me," inquired Marilyn, "what was Professor Rhoades doing with those federal agents/CIA guys this morning?

"He was with CIA guys?"

"Yeah, he landed on the big lawn in this black helicopter with two federal agents. Got Big John all upset and stuff."

"How did you know they were federal agents?"

"'Cause Big John said the pilot was so snotty and shoved this badge in his face. He was NYPD, he can tell. I think they like… threatened him or something."

"What did those agents look like?"

"I don't know; I wasn't that close, but the pilot was skinny and tall, the other one was kinda blond, same height as professor Rhoades."

"I see."

"See what, what do you see?"

"Oh, nothing; ok my love, I have to meet professor Rhoades for the session. I'll call you tomorrow," he kissed her on the cheek.

He arrived at professor Rhoades' office ten minutes before the agreed upon time. Professor Taggart was there alone on the phone. Taggart motioned him to sit while he concluded the phone conversation.

"Hi Lance, did you get a nap?"

"No, not really; I was too anxious I guess. Where are professor Rhoades and Miss King?"

"They're at the lab getting things ready, and I figured we would have time to talk for a while. You like her, don't you? That's OK; we're two guys talking. You should tell her, man; you may be the one after all."

"The one?"

"She's been all studies and career. The three of us have always looked young for our positions; Phil and I grew beards to appear older, but there was nothing physical Tina could do, so she developed a serious demeanor and a no-nonsense approach to forming relationships. It may cost me dearly if she knows I'm telling you this, but I've never seen her so loose around anyone else; I mean besides Phil and me. Something else, I don't think anyone has ever come up to her ideal. I see the way she talks to you, the way she looks at you; perhaps she feels the same way toward you."

"She likes me as a student; she is my teacher, she's the best."

"How old are you, Lance?

"Twenty two."

"Well, you're the same age; it doesn't matter that you're a student; we are an unconventional bunch, and besides, you have a very promising future ahead of you. But if you want to talk yourself out of contention... Anyway, you want to talk about our friend Spock, don't you?"

"Who?" Lance asked.

"You know... aw, stop it.

"Well, after this intro, I don't know if he is that important anymore. But okay, what have you found out professor? Has he told you who he really is?"

"You know, the funny thing, he knew I was going to insist as a condition of letting him in the loop. He called me after you left and told me that he works for the Israeli government, and that they want what legally belongs to them. They will let us have it for the next three months; we can take credit for our work if we succeed, then the tablet should be returned to the Israeli Museum."

"He's lying, this whole story is ridiculous; can't you see?" Lance almost screamed out.

"Hey! Take it easy, Lance, I've been doing this for years; governments can be fickle. With them, what's permissible today may be prohibited tomorrow."

"I'm sorry, but there are ways to verify this, aren't there? We should contact either the Israeli Museum, our state department, or whoever handles this kind of thing. I understand your impatience professor, but do you know that the man is CIA, or some kind of federal agent?"

"And you are certain of this?"

"Yes, yes I am. The school security chief can attest to it."

"If that's the case, what do we do?"

"Let's see what professor Rhoades thinks. Personally, I would like to proceed with the session; I'd like to see what kind of synergy we can establish."

"Oh, you can establish pretty good synergy, Lance, if you don't chicken out," said professor Taggart with a wink.

Lance looked at the professor with a confused expression, cocked his head like a pooch, and waited to grasp a meaning. Suddenly a big smile stretched out across his face.

"You mean... Come on Prof, you're trying to get me in trouble? Really, you think I have a chance? Oh! She is so... tell me professor, why haven't you or professor Rhoades made a play? I mean, she's so beautiful, so... hum, you know."

"We know, we know," sighed Taggart, "you see, we grew up together, the three of us, same neighborhood, same high school, same college; we were in love with her, as every red blooded heterosexual boy who ever laid eyes on her was. We competed for her company; we braved her father's wrath for the pleasure of walking her home from school. She never used us; I guess she realized that choosing one over the other would have meant wrecking our friendship. After a while, we became her older brothers; she became our younger sister to love and protect. We had been declared gifted, the three of us; we attended the best schools in the city. At fifteen, (she was thirteen) we were offered scholarships to every university. We stayed together until graduate school, and then I went to work at Georgetown University. It's too late now; our friendship would get in the way. Don't make the same mistake, don't let friendship creep in between the two of you; she is too easy to like."

They walked into the main lab room to find professor Rhoades and Tina rewiring and testing the equipment.

"She's technically inclined as well, isn't she," Lance marveled.

"Oh yeah, she is a genius; she can do it all, not just a pretty face and gorgeous bod," answered Taggart loudly.

"I can hear you," Tina sang.

"Well then, just say thank you like a cute little tomboy," said Taggart.

"Who are you calling little? Hi Lance," smiled Tina from across the room, "did you get some rest, we have work to do tonight."

"Yeah, a lot of sleeping, and hopefully dreaming," added Phil.

"Hey! What am I, invisible?" protested Taggart to Tina. Then turning to Lance, "you see what I mean? I guess you're the man now."

"Sorry Tag, I saw you only thirty minutes ago, you spoiled brat. OK, here," she kissed him on the cheek.

"So everything is alright? Taggart, Lance?" inquired Phil.

"Lance still has reservations, but he agreed that we should go ahead, boss; if you wish."

"Lance?" Phil prodded.

"Well, I learned that Mr. Spock is a government agent; there's something else about him that worries me even more. But we should go on with this; maybe, it will become clear in the morning.

"I think we should proceed as well. After all, our objectives are not limited to that subject alone. Everyone agrees?"

Everyone agreed. It was 9:00 PM, and everyone was in position. Lance, and Tina who turned out to be the other new recruit to the delight of Lance, were laid down, strapped, wired and glued to high tech ottomans, terminals, monitors, helmets and other strange devices. The helmets were fitted with wire-mikes to allow two-way communication. Before retiring in his booth behind the two-way-mirror/partition, professor Rhoades told them to relax by listening to their breathing, not to try to fall asleep, but to let it come naturally. Lance will be the leader; he will try to have a predetermined dream, which he has described and sealed in an enveloped in the possession of professor Rhoades. Tina should think about Lance as she falls asleep, and she should not concentrate on the sound of professor Rhoades' voice. The goal will be two-fold, dream initiating and dream sharing. No communication can be had between them upon awaking to preserve the integrity of the experiment. He then asked them whether they had something to say to one another.

"One thing," said Lance to Tina, "trust your judgment, let things happen, and try to remember details. One more thing, if you think it's me, it is."

"You mean four things," Tina giggled.

There was laughter as they settled in their positions. The lights were dimmed gradually in anticipation of somnolence. Lance took one more look at Tina before closing his eyes; his heart could not believe its good fortune.

The sun was just above the horizon when they exited the room. Phil was careful not too allow a long exposure to its rays as they quickly walked down the hallway. He believed that sunlight has a way of erasing the twilight's images from the mind. They entered the dimly lit conference room to the aroma of coffee and donuts that had been ordered the previous evening. As the sounds of sipping and chewing fill the air, Phil greeted everyone a good morning, thanked all for a great session, and then asked Taggart to open with his impressions of the night's proceedings.

"Guys, it was fantastic," he obliged with gusto, "I wish my people could have witnessed it. What a display of talent, professionalism, competence, and snoring I might add. I will tell you, there are some things that I only believed half way, but this morning, I am a true believer. I thank you, Phil, for allowing me to be an active participant in this. I'll give you back the floor before I spill the beans.

"I know I was not snoring, I never snore, must have been Lance," Tina complained.

"I heard it too, it was a lady's snore; you know, with a melody to it," Lance confirmed.

There was laughter, hands slapping by the men, and pouting by Tina.

"Oh Lance, what happened to being a gentleman and covering for a lady," she asked, slapping him on the arm.

"But I said it was a nice and melodious snore," Lance buttered.

"Nice try," Taggart laughed.

"OK," Phil interrupted, "it was a very successful session. We achieved both of our objectives with flying colors. I have transcripts of the post naptime interviews with Taggart and myself. As they were conducted independently, neither of you knows what was related by the other. The first dream occurred at 9:46 pm. Only Lance was observed dreaming. Upon awakening, he could not give an account. At 11:03 pm, both Tina and Lance displayed extensive and simultaneous REMs. The interview following revealed a dream about a church of some sort, lions gargoyles, and flying. Both Lance and Tina shared the same dream, from different vantage points it seemed. Nothing happened until 3:38 am when the monitors alerted us that something was taking place. It was to be an unusually long dream. Our dreamers awakened somewhat exhausted, but excited. They gave a fantastic account of a shared adventure that spanned several locales, actors, and plots. At this time, communication between subjects is permitted, and encouraged. I like to know to what extent recollection is comparable. Lance, would you give us a summary of the night's action."

"I do not recall the first dream that was recorded," Lance began, "but as you know, professor, there can be dreams without REMs or

REMs without dreams. Those are your flashes, your stills; the brain backfiring or rewinding I like to think. The first dream happens to be the one I wanted to initiate. By the way, I described it in the sealed note I handed you last night, professor. The location is a roman or Greek style temple; there are statues of lion's gargoyles on each side of the huge entrance. I find myself flying over a congregation; people throw things at me. I scoop down to within feet of their heads, some try to catch me; others try to hit me with whatever they have in their hands. I think I am with a bird."

"I saw the same thing," Tina added, "except that I was probably on the floor. I heard a conversation before you made that spectacular entrance. Funny, I knew that it was you. I felt as if we were in roman ruins that they were using as a meeting place."

"I agree," Lance concurred.

"Tina, would you summarize the last dream?

Miss King glanced in Lance's direction and started to laugh. She tried several times to begin her summary, to no avail. Lance, for his part, kept his eyes down, his gaze fixed on the table, a shy smile on his face.

"Lance then, would you?" Phil asked.

"No, no I'm ready," Tina insisted.

She took a deep breath, paused for a couple of seconds, and then began,

"We're walking down a long, deserted street. I can see the tops of houses and the sun about to rise; we reach the bottom of the hill, turn into a small street, and find ourselves in the middle of a group of young people. Lance is challenged to a fight; they don't like him for some reason. He asks me to stand against a house, while he fights one of them. Next, we find ourselves inside a room filled with technical devices. There's a telescope pointed toward the sky, and what can be described as a computer. I look at some notebooks. I think I recognize equations and various schematics and drawings. We leave in a hurry; someone is coming. We jump out of a window and land in tall bushes, and then we... I mean they..."

Tina's was again stricken with a case of the giggles. Lance joined in, as each turned away, unable to look at the other.

"Come on, they what?" insisted Phil.

"Can't you see?" Taggart asked, "Lance and Tina sitting in the bushes K-I-S-S-I-N-G... shame, shame, shame."

"Professor!" professor Rhoades chastised.

"I'm sorry, no shame, no shame; it's quite alright," joked Professor Taggart.

"He started it," Tina protested, pointing toward Lance.

"I didn't do it, it was whoever I was in," Lance defended.

"Come on, you saw an opportunity, and you took it, didn't you; you sly dog," Taggart dogged.

"I'm sorry," Lance apologized to Tina.

"It's alright," said Taggart, laughing.

"Excuse me, can I answer for myself? How do you know it's alright?" Tina cracked.

"You're saying it's not?" Taggart pursued.

There was no answer, but the sound of a knee hitting the underside of the table followed by a high pitch "ouch" meant that someone had just been punished with a kick to the shin. Inside of Lance's head, and echoing down his spine, the sound of drumbeats lead a choir to an exhilarating crescendo "*Halleluiah, halleluiah...*" he was thankful that the table was not made of glass.

"Changing the subject, did you get the impression...?"

Before Tina could finish her question to Lance, he reached over, put a hand over hers and an index finger on his own lips to signal her to stop speaking, and then loudly declared,

"Sorry, that was my stomach growling. I need some real food. I had no dinner last night. The diner on Steinwick should be open by now."

All understood that they had to leave the premises, and that he had something to reveal.

"Yeah, I could use something; let's get some fresh air," agreed Professor Rhoades."

Outside, twenty feet away from the lab-building front door, everyone stopped and turned toward Lance and waited for an explanation.

"Miss King, you started to ask me if I got the impression..."

"...that they were talking about Spock? Yeah, did you?"

"I was in the rafters, but I knew the concern was when Spock was coming back to lead them to the planet. It was not merely an impression, I knew."

"But wait a minute; is Spock some sort of a cult leader or something?" Taggart asked, "What planet? Why did we have to come out here? You think we're being bugged?"

"It crossed my mind when you said that he called right after your conversation with professor Rhoades, and then you told me that he called you as soon as I left. I'm not sure who or what he is yet. But if my suspicions are correct, your phone will ring within the next two minutes."

Lance checked his watch and everybody waited. The sound of a vibrating cell phone and a ring brought a gasp out of everyone. Taggart fumbled for his phone.

"Hum... who is this?" he asked incredulously, "... I'm tired, I've been up all night, I wouldn't recognize my mother's voice... no, I'm too exhausted, I'm going to have breakfast, and then get some sleep at a friend's, I'll call you when I'm ready to go back... I don't know, about 4:00 this afternoon I guess, I want to be in Washington tonight as well. Don't worry; I can take the train... Okay then, I'll call you when I'm ready to leave."

"Lance, you are something," marveled Taggart at Lance's feat.

"Oh, it's nothing. I knew that if he were listening to us, he'd become nervous about losing his connection; he'd want to know what we're up to."

"So, you were looking at a notebook of some sort, full of equations and drawings. There must have been some notations; could you make out the language?" Phil digressed.

"It seemed as if I could, but as soon as I became conscious I lost the images, only the certainty that I was looking at equations remained," Tina answered.

"Can I say something? Lance asked.

"That's why we're here," Phil answered.

"I have deduced from my experiences that when we dream, we are not speaking and hearing words. We're in a place between the brain and the ego, we intercept ideas or thoughts from the preconscious before the mental and conscious can be reached. I believe that's why we don't see the lips move, but we still think we hear because of conditioning. It would not matter the language; if either of us were a scientist or a mathematician, all he would have to do is induce one of them to read the notebook..."

"But I am a mathematician, my young friend, and professor Rhoades is a physicist," Tina informed.

"Well, *excusez moi,* I did not know that, and don't call me young, Miss King; I happen to know that I'm older than you," quipped Lance.

"Oh, really!" mugged Tina.

"Yeah, by... three, three and a half months," offered Lance.

"And how do you know that?"

"Well, I called your dad; he was cleaning his guns in case, you know... but I assured him that it was just a kiss in a dream, but that I would do the right thing nevertheless if anything... develops. He put the guns away, and we then had a pleasant talk; still, I felt it would be wise to decline the invitation to go hunting. I think he likes me now; he wants me to call him Dad."

That brought up a big volley of laughter, which took Taggart out of his uncharacteristic silence to inquire,

"Say Phil, could you put Tina under, see if she can recall those equations and drawings; there may be a connection. The spook said that his dreams hold the key..."

"Yes, we will try that," agreed Professor Rhoades.

The Kidnapping

"*P*rofessor, Professor, she's been kidnapped!*"

"Lance? Calm down... Who's been kidnapped?" inquired professor Rhoades, as he switched the receiver from one hand to the other, so that he could reach the lamp at the other end of his office couch on which he had just started to sleep, "why... did you witness this?"

"*We were leaving the coffee shop, she noticed that she had forgotten her bag; I offered to go back for it. I got to the entrance; I turned just in time to see her pushed into a car. They sped off before I could do anything. Oh! I feel so helpless! My god, who would... why? I called the police but...*"

"OK, they're going to take you to the police station. I'll meet you there."

Half way between the lab and the front gate, two men in dark suits stopped the professor.

"We are from OSID. Do not try to decipher it. It's a very covert national defense organization. We have little time; please, come with us. The life of your colleague depends on how fast we move." said one of the men.

They pointed to a black sedan parked on the other side of the street. As one of the men opened the back door, the figure in the back seat, cowering in a semi-fetus position against the tainted window, straitened up; it was Lance.

"They picked me up right after I hung up with you... This is what she was warning me about, professor," he blurted out.

"Tina? She warned you about this?"

"In a dream... she tried to warned me about something, a coming danger; I'm sure this was it," whispered Lance.

"Why didn't you tell us?"

"I didn't think..."

"From now on, everything is important," professor Rhoades accentuated with clinched jaw.

Before he could say another word, Lance put a finger on his lips and mouthed the "Shh" sound. He noticed the man in the passenger seat leaning to the left toward them, in an apparent effort to listen in on their conversation. They had not noticed that the partition had suddenly started to rise, sealing them from the front. Seconds later, a fog-like mist filled the compartment; they felt themselves sink into unconsciousness, unable and unwilling to struggle.

They awakened in a large, non-descript room; the absence of doors, windows, and ceiling lights gave them the impression of being inside a giant box. The room was brightly lit, but there did not seem to be a light source anywhere within the four walls, or on the ceiling. As they regained the ability to focus, they recognized their abductors; an equally stern looking man stood silently behind them.

"Good afternoon, gentlemen," said a voice from across the room. "We are somewhere near Washington D. C., the reason why will be clear in a moment. For now, I am agent B12, this is agent A9; behind us is Mr. Rotcod. Some people, with whom you are familiar, will join us shortly; in the meantime let's bring each other up to speed on what's been happening."

"Yeah let's," Lance seethed "we've been kidnapped, drugged, transported three hundred miles away like cargo, and my professor's been kidnapped by who knows who and for what; I say somebody needs to be brought up to speed! Don't you, professor?"

"Is this what a US citizen should expect from his government's agents? If that is what you really are," professor Rhoades added.

"Gentlemen you have not been kidnapped," the man introduced as Mr. Rotcod replied, "you've been taken away from a dangerous situation, and you were brought here to help us in a crisis, and to help us find your friend. When you hear what we have to tell you, you will be convinced that we are the good guys. We had to act as we did for the sake of expediency, and to circumvent our enemies' next move." "What enemies?" Rhoades fired back," "We are just college professors; Lance is our student working on a project of no importance to this or any other government. There is no situation."

"Not as far as you're aware," added A9, "but we had to be convinced that you were not willfully collaborating with foreign agents to undermine this country's interests. You call him Mr. Spock; we have reason to believe that he works as a double agent for the CIA, and the Chinese government. Anyone associated with him, like your friend, professor Taggart, and recently your group, professor Rhoades, and any project you're working had to be closely scrutinized, and we assume would be of interest to other agencies as well. Recent developments have proved us right."

"Then we can assume that you're in the process of arresting him, aren't you?" inquired professor Rhoades.

"Well, it's not that simple," agent B12 joined in, we have never observed him in contact with them, nor have we been able to assess an objective for a possible collaboration; although we know that both he and the Chinese have an interest in professor Rhoades' find from the Sinai."

"Why would they be so willing to provoke an international incident over an artifact of only archeological significance?" Lance asked.

"Ah yes, young man, that's the million-dollar nugget; why indeed?" echoed Mr. Rotcod. "We think you're on the right track, Lance, but we not he and his friends should be around when you get the answer."

"Wait a minute!" Rhoades stood up, "you've been bugging us all that time?"

"It seems that everybody's been listening in on you. Aren't you glad we crashed the party?" B12 Joked.

"Where were you when she was getting kidnapped?" Lance asked.

"We were out of sight for obvious reasons; we had not predicted such a bold and risky move of them. We intercepted your call to the police, but by that time the bad guys were gone, and we had no description or direction; you were too distraught to be coherent," A9 explained.

"So, what's going to happen to her now?" Lance wanted to know.

"We're waiting to hear from our contact; don't worry, she'll be returned; I promise you."

"You know," Rhoades stopped and shook his head in disbelief, "you are Intelligence, National Security, Home Land and all that other stuff, but it seems to me that you always know after the fact; after somebody's been kidnapped or killed, after the bombs have exploded, after the planes have been hijacked, after the terrorists have graduated from flying school and crashed the planes through the buildings; after, after, after..."

The two agents turned to look at Mr. Rotcod, as if to invite him to take the floor. It was a long list of blames, and informing their accuser that none of those cases had fallen under their jurisdiction would have only exacerbated matters. Rotcod took a deep breath, looked behind him for a chair, pulled up closer and started to speak.

"What I'm going to tell you, gentlemen, is classified information, some of which you may have read in the tabloids, and have been disavowed by our government, and part of which will be too fantastic even to scientists like you, professor Rhoades. Five years ago, the earth was stricken by a ray of light so strong that night was brighter than day for many countries in the Middle East. At ground zero, Israel was directly in the trajectory of the ray. The scientific community scrambled to come up with a plausible hypothesis. Theories ranged from a rogue nation's experiment with a space laser weapon, to gamma ray burst, to sun flare, to positronic lightning, a supernova, jet from a microquasar and its superluminal motion, and a half dozen other propositions. However, the phenomenon was benign; none of the effects that should have been observed in every proposed scenario was recorded by any of the observatories in that region; therefore, it remained unexplained. A few years later, the CIA received information that the Chinese had sent a team of archeologists to Israel, whose covert mission was to find what the aliens in that UFO had not recovered. See, they believed that the light phenomenon, years earlier, was the result of a spacecraft entering our atmosphere. They came looking for something they had left here on earth way back in ancient times. I guess it took them that long to return! They hadn't solved the problems of interstellar travel," he giggled.

"How did they come by this theory?" Lance posed, "I mean, they're not stupid,"

"Hey listen, some of our own scientists came to comparable suppositions; they were afraid to tarnish their reputation with published declarations. Some witnesses, Bedouins, soldiers, and even a very brave Israeli pilot reported that the light had consolidated into a disk, a UFO if you will, and was zipping around in the night sky over the desert. But to answer your question Mr. A-vig-non..."

"I'm sorry, it's Avi..." Lance started to object, "Never mind."

"It's common knowledge that our government has been working on a program to develop the use of ESP, astro-traveling, and dreams for spying. We know that the old Soviet Union had heavily invested in research in those fields. Well, gentlemen, the Chinese think they have reached the finish line. We have learned that they have a young mystic who can accomplish marvelous feats. We think that in the right environment and with proper techniques, you, Lance, can outdo him. We closed a similar program some years ago. By the way, your Mr. Spock was a very good prospect.

"So, what does he do now? Is he still with the CIA?" inquired Rhoades.

"Don't be so impatient professor, we want you to know everything; that will dictate how you proceed, once you team is together again," cautioned Rotcod.

"This is very riveting sure, but we need to go rescue Miss. King; you said it yourself, her life is in danger," Lance reminded the other two men.

"Yes! The FBI is waiting to hear from their contact, they're sure they'll be able to learn her exact location within the hour," B12 informed.

"Hour, Hour?" Lance almost screamed. "We can do better professor," he declared, looking at Rhoades.

"We can? Ah yes, we can… er, gentlemen, we need to be alone and we need a recording device and a map of the city," Rhoades demanded.

Rotcod and the two agents looked at each other, hesitated, suddenly unsure of their roles.

"Take away these walls and ceiling!" Rhoades ordered.

Nothing happened.

"What?" Lance looked at the professor, perplexed, wondering whether the sleeping mist had done damage to his brains.

"Do you really want us to help you as you said, or are we under arrest? Which is it?" Rhoades pressed on defiantly.

There was an additional moment of silence and hesitation then,

"No! you're free to stay or go as you please," Rotcod said, and then turned to the wall behind him, "Go ahead, do what the man said," he ordered.

The walls started to undulate, and then gradually fade to reveal a large vestibule around which various offices and closed rooms were arranged in a rectangle. Up above, in the center of the ceiling, a monster size projector looked on, poised to deliver all manners of hologram images at the touch of a button.

"Over here, gentlemen" said B12.

They were directed to a small conference room where awaited everything Rhoades had requested. Once the door had been closed, Lance turned to Rhoades and whispered,

"How did you know it was a hologram? I..."

"It was all too perfect. The walls, no light source, the light distribution too even, no shadows; didn't you notice? Listen, what in heaven are we doing here? Sure you can do this?"

"Oh yeah! We're going to try for her sake, professor, and we're going to succeed," Lance promised.

He sat in the comfortable armchair at the head of the table, leaned back, and then announced,

"I'm ready professor, do your thing!"

The Rescue

"Remember, once we get off that exit, there should be a large street; we have to make a right... no, a left," directed Lance, "I have this problem, professor, when I awaken from a dream, everything is turned around; what was left in the dream is actually right, up turns out to be down; it's strange."

It remained an unsolvable problem for Lance – at least intellectually. He reasoned that perhaps the super-ego does not transmit information to the brain via an analogous mechanism; there is not always symmetry in the translation. Perhaps, he further posited, he has not yet developed the metaphysical modem necessary for unscrambling data logically from the dream realm to the here and now. Nevertheless, it seems that the message comes through the distortions with enough impact to be recognized – when it needs to be.

"Don't worry, Nostradamus," joked B12, "The professor has a map, we have GPS; we'll find the place. Besides, those FBI boys are familiar with it. They have had it on radar for some time, under suspicion of trafficking or something. Now they have kidnapping and transporting across state line to add to the list."

"They have jurisdiction, but they know this is our case. She'll come with us when it's over," added A9.

"Let's pray that she'll be there when we get to the place! I mean that she won't be moved..." Lance worried.

"They have a couple of undercovers watching it for anything suspicious; just a few more minutes, Mr. A-vee- yon," A9 took his time pronouncing Lance's last name.

"I'll go in first ;" Lance informed "I'll try to remember everything, but just in case, if I go right, send somebody left; if I go up, send somebody down. And..."

"They understand, guy," Rhoades said in a soft voice, "lay back, close your eyes and visualize; it'll all be ok."

Minutes later, they pulled in front of a video game parlor, followed by an FBI and DC police escort. Lance was first out of the van, with the two agents and Rhoades in tow. Inside, they waited for the FBI to catch up while apologizing to the manager for the unannounced visit; still, they would like his permission to tour the establishment, hoping, of course, that it would not be too much of an inconvenience. Some reticence was perceived but not communicated. Once the FBI agents and police had reached, Lance led them straight to the rear of the noisy and crowded lobby and opened a door. A long dimly lit staircase led down to a large gambling room. A huge man in dark clothing approached the bottom step to see what the commotion was, or to dispatch quickly any undesirables; he got an FBI badge shoved in his face. He jumped backward either to gain distance for a better look, or out of an occupationally developed instinctive aversion to badges. A careful search of the premises turned up nothing. Suddenly, Lance remembered something,

"The bathroom!" he yelled, "That's what it was, the bathroom!"

"We looked in there, there's nothing...," someone said.

Before anyone else could react, he ran across the room and opened the door with the restroom sign. The sound of stalls doors slamming echoed throughout the basement. Finally, he slowly shuffled out, a defeated man, beating himself over the head with both hands, tears streaming down his face, and muttering "I don't understand, I don't understand" over and over. All, veteran FBI agents and police detectives, even a few of the gambling patrons, had lumps in their throats, and were fighting back tears. Agent B12 approached him, put an arm around his shoulders, and whispered,

'We'll try again, and we'll leave no stone unturned; we'll find her!"

"No stone unturned... Thank you, thank you!" Lance embraced him, turned away, and then ran back to the restroom, leaving B12 to wonder,

"Oh no! What did I do? What did I say?"

"He's lost it," said an FBI man.

"Get him outta there!" A9 ordered.

They opened the door to find the back wall of the middle stall pushed open to reveal a concealed room. The toilet bowl wearing an 'out of order' sign was turned around and laid to one side, and they heard the sound of a fight in progress. Lance was on his back in a break-dance position, and resembling that species of spiders that fight on their backs. He was kicking, spinning, caching an opponent's head, leg, or arm between his and pulling him to the ground, and then flipping on his hands and knees to pounce on him. The next second, he was on his back performing the completely strange exhibition all over again. When he was done, and the two men were stretched out unconscious on the floor, he flipped back on hands and knees and sprang up to a more natural bipedal posture. Spectators, silent, open mouthed, and stocked up in the small opening, were not sure whether what they had just witnessed was real. Someone, a young woman in a dark corner of the room suddenly exclaimed,

"What in the name of Jackie Chan was that, Lance?"

"Miss. King! Are you all right?" Lance shouted. He ran over, kissed her, kissed her again, and... well, he would have kissed her perhaps a dozen more times, if the pile-up at the small opening had not collapsed. Agents and cops were sliding and rolling across the floor.

"I'm ok, considering... What took you so long?" demanded Tina.

"Ok... we were taken to some..."

"Are you going to untie her?" Professor Rhoades wanted to know, "Or perhaps it's more convenient for you that she remains like this."

The room exploded with laughter.

"Oh! I'm, I'm sorry! I didn't mean to... really, I was just so..."

"Oh Lance, stop it already," Miss. King chastised. She then turned and whispered in his hear,

"Thank you, my hero...perhaps another time."

A Concerned Taggart

"Good evening professors, good evening Lance, and welcome back from the land of Arachnia. I'm so sorry I missed that exhibition," Mr. Rotcod smiled, as everyone assembled in the screening room looked in Lance's direction.

"I'm sorry I missed the kiss," professor Taggart added, provoking an outburst of laughter and whistling.

"Where did you learn to fight like that?" Rotcod inquired

"I don't know... never fought anyone before." Lance answered.

At that point, someone started to sing the old Huey Lewis song, *"That's the Power of Love."*

"For God's sake, Taggart, be serious for once," implored Tina, "there is national security stuff at stake here." and then she added, "Jealous!"

"Yes I am! Here he comes with his boyish charm and good looks, and his gift of dreaming or something. He didn't make the greatest find of the century, I did. Listen, I got the CIA, the FBI, and these guys here fighting over me, so dream on, spider-man. You can have the girl this time, but we will meet again; I'll be back!"

No one, outside of the four of them, knew what to make of Taggart's apparent outburst until the almost perfect rendition of Arnold Schwarzenegger's line "I'll be back" loosened the perplexed brows. Then a big volley of laughter broke loose. Mr. Rotcod waited for the hilarity to subside, and then said,

"Some of you have been brought here incognito because this is still an ultra-secret government facility, and we are now working on a similarly designated project. We had no time to get everyone proper security clearance, however, you will be held accountable for any breach, and subjected to the same retribution as the rest of us would be. Now, for those of you not aware of the day's news, an attempt has been made to break into professor Taggart's office in order to appropriate his famous artifact and relevant records. As we have anticipated such an action, we took the liberty of removing the object of contention to a safer location. Other agencies wanted custody of it, but we won out; as soon as you resume your work, we will make it available to you. You see, professor Rhoades, we can beat the bad guys to the punch once in a while. We had no time to transfer your individual labs and equipment here. However, I'm sure you will find our facility here more than adequate. Our own scientists, engineers, and experts in various fields will join you. They are more familiar with our capabilities, and therefore they will compliment you nicely. Professor Rhoades, you will forgive us for having reproduced your device; our scientists have made some amelioration and added some applications that I'm sure will meet your approval. It is still your invention; we have gotten you a patent in your name. Professor Taggart, the full power of our data processing apparatus, technicians included, is at your service. You'd like to add something Professor Rhoades?"

"I'd like to remind everyone that this is first and foremost a scientific and academic project. The four of us duly appreciate this agency, the FBI, CIA, and others saving our butts. In as much as the success of our research is not used in a way that is in conflict with our ethics and values, but contributes to the advancement of science and its goal of improving the human condition, our cooperation will be well served."

"Professor Taggart, professor King, Mr. Avignon, would you like to add something?" asked Mr. Rotcod.

The three signaled a 'no' answer with headshakes.

"Then we will reassemble in the 'War Room' for a proper 'greet and meet' and disposition of assignments."

"Excuse me sir, before we do, the four of us would like to have a little summit," Taggart announced.

"Ok then, I'll send someone for you in… say fifteen minutes?"

All but the four exited the small theater. Then Taggart, still seated and looking straight ahead, spoke,

"Phil, why do you presume to give our consent? I agreed to come here because I heard what happened to Tina. I don't know about Tina or Lance, but being enrolled in some secret government program is not my favorite thing in the world. Did you hear him? *"As soon as you resume your work, we will make it available to you."* you know what that implies, don't you, we'll let you see it, if you decide to work for us. How do we know they didn't set this whole thing up from the beginning? You remember what Lance said about the artifact having some kind of power. It wouldn't surprise me that they're considering a military application…"

"Come on Tag, don't start…"

"Don't start! It's already started. Did you hear him; *you'll be held accountable for any breach, and subjected to the same retribution.* When did I take an oath for spy or secret service duty? We are educators, for Christ's sake, we have whole departments to run, or have you forgotten? Get a hold, man!"

"Hey, hey, don't put that on me, Professor!" Phil fired back, "I was running my department! I was content to conduct my very mundane research in peaceful anonymity. But who came flying in with his big fancy helicopter, with his federal agent buddy, and Indiana Jones tale, huh? I wouldn't have said it, but you got us in this mess. Have you even apologized to Tina for what she had to go through?"

"Phil, it's ok, really," Tina interceded.

"No, it's not ok. He's too busy worrying about his precious artifact to bother," Phil added.

"I'm so very sorry Tina! You know how precious you are to me... to us. Maybe you're right Phil, I'm too self-absorbed. I simply thought..."

"I know! I could have been more considerate of your input as well. Tina, Lance anything you want to say?" asked Phil in a more conciliatory tone.

"He's sleeping! Can you believe it?" Taggart said as he pulled one of Lance's eyelids open.

"He's had a long day," Tina said, "we all have; perhaps we should postpone tonight's experiment."

Suddenly, Lance awakened and jumped on his feet after uttering a big "Wow!"

"What... something?" Phil asked.

"Something alright, big something!" Lance replied, "We have to make a recording of it while it's still fresh in my head. Let's go!"

"Where?" Tina asked.

"To the spider cage!" Lance shouted.

"What spider cage? Anybody knows what he's talking about?" Taggart asked.

"I've seen that look before, we'd better go. Follow him!" was Phil's advice.

With Lance leading, they exited into a long corridor, at the end of which an imposing set of double doors seemed to indicate that important personnel only could enter. Lance went through them as if he had done it countless times before. Inside, the unmistakable glare of computer screens, the sea of desks and chairs and other devices, and the four story high map of the world left no doubt, it was the War Room.

"How did he know?" Taggart marveled.

"He's Lance," was Tina's simple answer.

A glass cage had been constructed up front below the giant screen to allow the experiment to be conducted in silent intimacy. Lance found a door, entered, and sat in one of the dentist-chair-like contraptions while Tina took the other,

"Professor, Miss. King, let's do it," Lance said.

A couple of technicians came in and, without saying a word, got to the task of connecting various devices to the subjects' heads, arms, and hands. In less than a minute, and under the professor's guidance, Lance and Tina had fallen asleep. Outside, on the main floor, Mr. Rotcod was signing orders; his left hand directing the lights to dim, while his right hand pointed at the big screen which came alive with a million little points of lights, appearing and disappearing, streaking then floating, until images started to take shape. They were eyes. Eyes so large they overflowed onto the ceiling, the floor, and the sidewalls; conquering, controlling eyes that seemed to want to penetrate everyone's soul.

"Detach yourself, be a spectator, be a listener," Professor Rhoades whispered to Lance.

The intensity subsided almost instantly, and the image shrunk to within the confines of the screen. The sound of a high-pitched uninterrupted whistle was heard. The screen went blank; the room became silent, and everyone looked exhausted. Inside the glass cage, professor Rhoades brought Tina and Lance back from their somber.

"What was that; what did we get?" Rotcod's voice impatiently boomed out of the small speaker, "Is that it?"

"Yep, That's it," answered Rhoades, "that was a long dream, now we have to play it back to our speed, and see whether our translator has done the job."

"Oh, right... How long was that, about five, six seconds? Then we slow it up to about 3,600 times? What do you think professor?" Rotcod asked.

"Should be about right." Rhoades agreed.

Rotcod gave the order to slow the speed of the playback. The sound of words being spoken was heard.

"Try it at 4,200," suggested Rotcod.

It was clear; a voice deep and majestic spoke. It sounded like a bible verse,

"In the beginning was the light, and the light was with God. Trough him everything came into being and without him nothing that exists came into being. The keeper of the light is here. It must be returned at the end of the next light cycle or the city within which it is held will be isolated from the rest, return it to the mountain with the messenger."

"Okay... Does anyone understand what that was about? Professor Rhoades, Lance?" Rotcod urged.

Tina was first to speak,

"Anyone familiar with Sunday school, no? Well, the first part of that statement refers to the creation if you're a believer or to the big bang if you subscribe to that theory. From what Lance and I have been able to ascertain, they are experimenting with light, and we think the artifact is the key to further discoveries. Earlier, we took a trip to a familiar destination, and we have been able to scope out the science behind it. It's quantum physics at its highest. We would need professor Rhoades' help for recall. We believe the keeper of the light is Mr. Spock, if he... well, not he, but the alien that has taken possession of his body and controlled his mind, if he is not released by the next light cycle... Lance?"

"The light cycle is one solar revolution; I should say one earth spin. I believe we are given 24 hours to let him and the artifact go. The object, I think, is a kind of data storage device that contains very advanced scientific knowledge. Professor Taggart came upon it before they were able to retrieve it."

"I would like a one on one with Mr. Spock," Said professor Taggart. "On our way into DC, I had the feeling that he was about to reveal something, perhaps a lead or a clue; but he was taken away as soon as we landed and I was brought here. I assumed those guys were FBI. When will we be able see him?"

Mr. Rotcod slowly walked up and down the main aisle, deciding how or whether to answer Taggart's question. Finally, he said,

"Mr. Spock, as he is known to you, is a CIA agent. As a rule, I do not discuss other agencies matters with non-agency personnel, but this is an unusual case, and you are an unusual group. Listen, these guys have work to do, going over this new system and this new data; let's go back to the conference room."

As they started down the mysterious corridor, Taggart whispered to Phil,

"There's no turning back now! Don't we make an unusual A-Team?"

Phil laughed silently. He laughed at the way Taggart could always find lightheartedness in any situation.

"Nothing new," he replied, "we have always been an unusual group, haven't we?"

"Yeah, but this new guy here really gives me the creeps!"

The Chief

CIA headquarters did not seem as bright on that day; the hallways had a cavernous quality in the way they echoed every minute sound, and the elevator maintained a deliberately slow downward slide inside its seemingly bottomless shaft. Spock had to summon all of his usual impassiveness to appear unconcerned; he was being lead to the Chief, the all-powerful, the mind reader, the ultimate... er, testicles buster. If the Chief knows it, it must be Truth. There is no room in his all-perfect dominion for falsehood, no time for allegations, and no patience for hearsay. To be summoned for an inquest means two things: you have something earth shattering to add to his Vastness, or... well, have that long and all revealing talk you have been meaning to have with the wife and kids; it's bad! The other two agents stayed in the elevator as they showed him the lone door straight ahead. With barely a sound, the elevator took off, leaving him alone to face the very ornate mahogany door and the blue water cascade on his left. He approached the door; he opened the door. As he crossed the doorway, he felt a jolt; he sensed heat leaving his body in one silent whoosh!

"Come in agent Novitz," said a voice from the other side of the big leather armchair facing the wall on the right side of the room, "I will tell you what I know; you will tell me what you know. You may answer some questions, and then you may leave. You will be told by other than myself what our disposition will have been. Do you understand?"

"Yes I do, sir."

The chair swiveled to face him, revealing a man of regular stature and a face as expressionless as one in the Grant Wood's painting, *American Gothic*.

"For a long time, agent Novitz, you were and still are, one the best operatives this agency has had. You were known and admired by all, friends and foes alike. You conducted successful operations on every continent in spite of that recognition, which is no easy feat. However, success often attracts envy and jealousy. They will dream up the most nefarious reasons to justify the fact that you can accomplish what they cannot. I believed in you, agent Novitz, as did my predecessor; you remember him. We spoke often and admiringly of you; you reminded him of himself as a young operative trotting the globe on the most dangerous of missions. It was not safe for you anymore; every foreign agent and his bureau wanted to make a name for himself by catching you with your hand in the kitty jar. They would have been willing to frame you, and some so-called friends of this country would have been happy to help them. So you see, we were delighted to have convinced you to enroll in that AIG initiative. You had the talent, and we wanted to see it at work. As you know, the Russians were investing a lot in a similar program of theirs, and there were rumors that they were having considerable success with remote viewing, which made some people around here very nervous. Unfortunately, someone thought that our results were too unreliable; successes were not predictable enough, and for what we were investing, the returns were meager at best. This agency did not make the decision, nor did we have the last word in closing the division. Nevertheless, it seems that everything you have done since has been an effort to express your bitterness and disappointment.

You could have been here imparting your knowledge and experience to young upcoming agents. We gave you time to vent because you had given so much to this agency. It's time to come back, agent Novitz; we need you now. Tell me what happened in Israel."

Spock paused, took a deep breath, cleared his throat, and then,

"Sir, three months before the closing of the unit, I told my section chief about a dream I had, involving a group of Chinese men digging in the desert. They were looking for a weapon that would make China the most powerful nation on earth. I saw myself being chased, captured, interrogated, and submitted to some kind of invasive procedure. But, I tell you sir, it was more precognition than it was a dream; I have learned to differentiate between the two. I wanted a promise that someone would consider looking into it, but I was derided. I could not understand; that was the goal of the study, to uncover stuff like that through our Alternative Intel Gathering approach. And to make it worse, the program folded. The opening for an attaché at the Israeli embassy was quite fortuitous..."

"It was my idea," The chief interrupted.

"Sir?"

"We did not want to, nor could we give legitimacy to a mission based on such a premise, and we wanted you to keep a low profile without making it an order, which would have incited you to be more defiant, given your mental disposition at the time."

"Then you knew, Sir that I was going to pursue my... hunch?

"I was counting on it.?"

"Well Sir, nothing happened for the first 3 months. Then the ambassador was invited to a function at the Chinese embassy. While there, I met an old friend, an ex KGB agent turned attaché like myself. We talked about the good old days of espionage; we compared the dynamics of the superpowers of old to those of the new powers of today, the so-called developing countries. As an example of the ease with which he now can distinguish between a spy and a real civil servant, he pointed to a Chinese man wearing a most identifiable university professor garb, who was going around the room introducing himself as an archeologist. We had the best laugh we have had in years of knowing each other. Toward the end of the night, it hit me: the dream, the desert, the dig! So, I began to follow the supposed Chinese professor."

"Where does professor Schaffhausen fit in all this," the chief inquired.

"He found what they were looking for; they intended to kill to acquire it. I did not know who the professor was at the time, but I could tell that they were Americans and they were going to be murdered. I got two of the four Chinese, but they had machine-guns against my M16. The Americans had gotten the message that it was time to get out of there, and I had drawn the Chinese fire, so it was my time to say goodbye. I reached the main road just in time to catch one in the front tire. The jeep flipped a few times; I blanked out. I do not remember anything after that. But I can assure you, Sir, I did not break and enter the embassy; I was not caught on embassy ground. I have since read the reports, I can see how..."

"Agent Novitz, you do not have to plead your case to me; I believe you. I believe you did the job we expected you to do. Thanks to you, Americans' lives were spared and we, not they, have the artifact. We do not know what it is yet, and why they wanted it so badly, but we will. You may stand down now, agent; we have people working at solving this. Your job is done. Once again, Congratulations, agent Novitz!"

"Thank you for the opportunity Sir!"

"I know you want to see this thing to the end, and as a favor to me, I would like you to join those guys and help them with what you know. As you have already found out, the young man, Mr. Avignon, has abilities comparable to your own; he can use your experience."

"Yes Sir,"

"We have learned some things about your stay with the Chinese. I want you to gather yourself; now slowly turn around and look at the door through which you entered."

"What the... is that's an invisible man, Sir?" Spock blurted out.

"Do not worry, he cannot see or hear anything, he might as well be in a cement box. What did you feel when you step through the door?

"As if I my body had received an electric shock and heat had suddenly left my body all at once. But I thought I was being nervous or apprehensive; you mean... that's me, Sir?"

"No, agent Novitz, that's not you. What you felt was he being yanked out of you. Mr. Rotcod, whom you will meet later, advised us to build what is but not entirely an electromagnetic cage that would be undetectable to him... and you. He had become so much a part of you that you would have done anything to protect him, and he you. Let us go back to your capture by the Chinese; they had planned to interrogate you, perhaps torture you, but you never came out of the coma that ensued following the rollover. When we discovered that they had you, they denied it; then they claimed that you had broken into their embassy, jumped out of a window upon being discovered, and suffered head trauma. While negotiations were under way for your release, we sent in a team of neurologists and surgeons; they reported that they were unable to find a cause for the coma, and that no trauma site could be identified. However, the moment you were placed inside the plane for your return trip, you opened your eyes and asked for something to drink. My friend let me tell you, you became more of a legend when rumors circulated around here that you had been able to fake a coma for three months to avoid interrogation and torture. However, the good feelings did not last long, as you became increasingly detached, surly, and gave the impression that you were, and I quote, better than the rest of us, unquote. Among many theories for your change of temperament was that you had turned double, or that they had surgically implanted some kind of spy gadget in your brain; both proved to be false."

"So, where does he... it come in the picture?" interrupted Spock?

"Mr. Rotcod is the eastern regional director of OSID. He was one of us ten years ago. I knew him, and he knew the old man. We had dinner one evening; I was telling him about the problem we faced with you not playing well with others recently. He stopped me in the middle of my account to declare that he knew what might be happening with you. He had designed a device to trap foreign entities that are able to co-habitate our bodies and our minds. He claimed to have used it successfully in at least two cases, and he wanted me to try it with you. Meet your alter ego for the past five years! I suspect he entered you while you were unconscious after the crash and he, not you, feigned the coma. I expect there is a connection with your investigation of the professor's research."

"Wow! Unbelievable!" was all Spock could utter.

"You cannot go out through that door, you will be double again. See that green dot on the left side of the door; touch it."

Spock did. The frame came up just enough to fill the one-inch gap above the top traverse, slid out and continued across the room to the opposite wall. The green shadow inside became agitated, having sensed movement, and was turning alternately gray, brown, and yellow.

"This will be known to only the three of us, You, Mr. Rotcod, and me. From now on, you answer directly to me. Craig, I expect you back in this office when this is over."

"Yes Sir!" Spock boomed.

"Len."

"Excuse me Sir!"

"My name is Len, you can call me Lenny. The old man called me Lenny. He was right; you do remind me of him, which is an honor Craig, an honor... I wish you had known him!" the Chief sighed as he looked over at the portrait of his predecessor on the opposite wall.

Spock took a long look at the man in front of him, There was nothing special about his appearance; his clothes belied that aura of power built around his persona. But there was something behind those eyes; an indefinable force, an energy at once overpowering and benign that commanded fear and fondness in the same instant; in the same impulse. Spock had an overwhelming urge to thank the man for allowing him to be in his presence; he wanted to shake the emperor's hand and physically feel the might, but neither of those acts was in the directives.

"Ok Craig, I will see you soon," the chief finally said.

"I will see you soon, Sir... er, Lenny."

They exchange a reserved smile, and Spock headed out. Upstairs, on the main operations level, he was regarded with surprise and awe. The man who survived capture, and evaded interrogation and torture by feigning coma for three months has now returned unscathed from the 'underworld' of Him.

"You're back! I... er, we thought..." rambled the first man who saw him, "how was... he?"

"Who, the chief?" Spock deadpanned, "He looks all right; only thing is he smiles too much. I told him people may not take him seriously. A man in his position can be only so pleasant, if you know what I mean!

"What?" exhaled the man, dumfounded.

Spock Incorporated

"As I was saying, Mr. ... er, Spock is a CIA agent; he has been almost from the beginning..." Mr. Rotcod recapped.

"Yeah, He looks it," Taggart interrupted.

"What do you mean?" asked Rotcod.

"He looks like he just came down the mountain with Moses in the beginning, you know... the bible. Tell them Tina."

"When Moses came down the mountain with the 10 commandments after his meeting with God, he looked so pale and strange that the Hebrews had problem recognizing him... God, anybody reads the bible!" Tina exclaimed.

"Wait, how far is that mountain from the spot where you found the artifact, professor Taggart?" Lance asked.

"A hundred kilometers, give or take," Taggart answered. "Why? You think..."

"I see!" Tina realized, "*Return it to the mountain with the keeper*; that's the mountain! Moses went up the mountain, he saw a burning bush, and he heard the voice of God speaking through it."

"The burning bush is the light," Lance shouted simultaneously with Tina, who continued,

"A bright object emitting light, in those days of no man-made, artificial light, could only be fire, and if it is behind a bush, it becomes a burning bush which, I might add, was never consumed by the fire."

There were applause, cheers, and head rubbing, and chanting of Tina's name.

"And the keeper was the voice we heard; the same voice that spoke to Moses." Taggart added.

There was silence!

"What, no props?" Taggart complained.

He got an "Oh, poor baby" from Tina.

"I think you have got something. However... er, excuse me." Rotcod asked, and then walked away to answer his pager unit. "What do we have? ... Yes, bring him in."

He turned toward the four to announce,

"Your Mr. Spock is here; he has gone through a... let's call it a procedure to remove an alien Spirit that had taken him over for the past few years. However, he has been himself at the same time. You may not think that I am serious, but judge for yourself. He is on his way; make him feel welcome."

Rotcod went out to meet Spock. The room became silent; there were sideways looks and raised brows. After a few agonizing minutes, the door opened and a tall, skinny but robust man entered, followed by Rotcod. The man offered a hand to Taggart who stood up and practically came nose to nose before noticing the other man's gesture of salutation. They shook hands, and then Taggart prodded,

"Spock?"

"Yes," confirmed the thin man.

"What happened? You're practically..."

"Reborn, pink again, Homo sapiens, exorcized?" Spock bantered.

"Hum... yeah!" Taggart mumbled.

Mr. Rotcod approached and started to introduce the rest of them.

"Weren't you the helicopter pilot?" Phil asked.

Rotcod got to Lance who already had a big smile on his face.

"I'm sure we met before; you were running away from me. You don't seem as shy this time around." Lance said.

"Well, let's just say that I wasn't myself. I'm sure you know what I mean." Spock smiled back.

"You two want to fill us in," Rhoades broke in, "you've never met before, have you?"

"I did not tell you because I wasn't sure until now," Lance answered. "We met in a dream, remember; that's why I felt uneasy about the professor's association with him. I wasn't just seeing him; I was also seeing the entity that had taken him over."

"I guess you're not Mr. Spock anymore," inquired Taggart, "I presumed that was his choice."

"No, I always liked Spock; he was my idol growing up. It was your choice for me professor, and it served me well, as do all my other aliases; I needed to be incognito, as I was when I saved your... sitting appendage and your excavating group in the desert."

"It was you?" Taggart exclaimed, "Wow, Phil, it was him! Man, we talked about that all the time. For a long time I was Indiana Jones, dodging bullets and getting away with the prized artifact. You haven't mentioned how you... I guess you were taking a walk in the desert that evening and decided to save fellow Americans in peril."

"Yeah, just like that." Spock laughed.

"The man has a sense of humor; that's not Spock-like," Taggart remarked.

"Mr. Spock," Tina interrupted the laughter, "we were having a discussion that you may find interesting, giving your past but recent merger with a certain being. Your input will carry greater weight if you are able to recall your experiences during that time."

"I'm glad to hear you call it a merger, Miss. King," Spock began, "because it was not your classic case of possession. The being needed me with my memory and personality intact and unaffected as an official of the government privy to information and knowledge he could use. What he did not intend, or perhaps he was impervious to, was that I would acquire his memory as well. Facts, events, and places in my dreams were feeling more and more like experiences of my own, with colors, clarity, and texture closer to those of this realm than to the nebulous qualities of our subconscious minds images. I was having recollection of a dream while dreaming. I know things I have never learned, I can do things I have never done or practiced. But it all felt normal; I could not tell anyone, I would have been deemed unstable. I felt myself changing, but I felt justified. I was different, I was misunderstood; I know now that I was under the alien's influence. They were obviously his dreams and his thoughts; not mine."

"I wonder Mr. Spock," professor Rhoades inquired, "to the extent that you can differentiate yours from his, whether you are able to recall his purpose, his mission… as a matter of fact, can you delineate chronologically or otherwise the history of his species? Well, insofar as it relates to the matter at hand. I have a feeling that's where some answers may lie."

"Yes" Spock agreed, "I have been able to organize those snippets of dreams and odd bits of acquired recollection into a somewhat continuous and coherent account. However, it seemed to span such an interminable amount of time and periods that I thought I was faced with stories from my own past consecutive lifetimes. Now I understand that it was not the case. I will try and keep it germane to our exploration."

"Yes Mr. Spock," Taggart interrupted, "pardon my impatience, can you progress it toward his interest in the artifact. We all agree that…"

"And you're right, professor Taggart. I'm sure Mr. Avignon will not mind helping me where I may falter some. He was there in more than a few of those… episodes."

"Only in the past few years," Lance opined.

"Not necessarily," Spock differed, "as you must know, dreams don't always follow a timeline."

"True! Ok… if I can," Lance promised.

Spock began,

"A long, long time ago, in a democracy far, far away, science reigned supreme. There was almost nothing thought or imagined that could not be accomplished. The humanities also flourished; democracy reached its pinnacle in theory and in practice, which made it easy to control greed and selfishness. It sounds like utopia, but it was real. Unfortunately, it is the universal way of evil to confound the good and well meaning by hiding behind a mask of religious devotion. Those few mask-wearers convinced a large minority that science would spell the end of their world. They needed to go back to the way of nature; to the beginning. They preached that God is the light, and that only God gives light; to manipulate light is to usurp God's authority. God will not allow it; he will destroy their species. Those demagogues were at war with the scientists for having gone too far, for altering the workings of nature, and for playing God, as they put it. They were not unlike your eartbound-pistols-packing-bible-carrying-hate-monger-ing-so-called-Christian-fundamentalists.

By a fluke of statistical anomaly, their candidate was narrowly elected, and soon, wholesale changes went into effect. Democracy was repealed; science and technology became the domains of government. There were no schools, scientific research was outlawed, and the arts were strictly censored. Anything a child needed to know, or would have ever known was implanted via the equivalent of a chip directly in his brain and upgraded at specific times during his development. Genetic manipulation ensured that the demands of the state were met in the kinds of individuals that comprised society. Nothing was left to chance; certain undesirable traits, tendencies, or ambitions that would not satisfy the needs of the state were artificially suppressed during childhood."

"Are we to expect a similar fate when they invade earth?" Mr. Rotcod wondered.

"In a word, no! You see, they lack the ability, or the desire to invade other planets. Remember, they're against science and technology."

"Then, how did he get here?" asked professor Rhoades.

"Space bike?" Taggart suggested with a raised hand.

He only got an amused smile from Lance. Mr. Rotcod stepped in front of the group, and with a serious tone reminded them that,

"There is only about 22 hours left; we've been given an ultimatum, if you remember. Go ahead, agent."

"You will understand in a minute, professor Rhoades. Where was I… yes, a group of scientists and artists who had seen the writing on the wall, and other farsighted free thinkers had decided to prepare for the worst. Early into the new regime and before the restrictive measures were implemented, they moved to a sparsely populated region where research facilities had been built to accommodate every branch of science. Artists, philosophers, technicians, artisans, and others who had feared that the intolerant faction would be a dire threat if it ever came to power, were invited to join. They were well insulated against attacks by land or by air. However, attempts at penetrating their defense never ceased, to the point where they began to foresee a day when they would be invaded and assimilated by force. They had to come up with an answer. Some of their physicists had been working on a project called the 'Travel Light;' they collaborated and had one built in record time.

The Travel Light, as I understand it, is the use of light for propelling an object such as a spaceship into outer space. They solved the problem of interstellar travel using light as propulsion. It is predicated on the premise that only light can travel faster than the speed of light. If you shoot a beam of light while you are traveling on a beam of light, the second beam will travel faster; there is no friction or recoil. By repeating this process, you can achieve incrementally faster than light speeds and bypass laws of physics that earth scientists hold to be forever unbreakable. They found a way to reconstitute matter itself and bring it back to the second manifestation of existence, light; conscience, thought, or knowledge having been the first. The prevailing assumption is that time itself becomes a non-factor when matter is synthesized down to thought or conscience. In other words, thought, or conscience is free of the constraints of time, having preceded time in the entire scheme of universal actualization. For now, they are able to turn both the ship and its occupants into photonic entities that can be integrated seamlessly in the travel light sequence. He is not a physicist; he is an artist and a philosopher, and he does not perceive the intricacies of the mathematical and scientific processes involved.

Their science is millenniums ahead of ours, and their philosophy does not permit them to kill. Their reason for coming here is to retrieve the tablet, which contains their accumulated knowledge and history. They have hidden it here on earth for safekeeping before the takeover at the time of Moses wonderings in the desert, to whom they entrusted it inside the tablets of the commandments. We know what happened; Moses broke them in a rage against the sinning Hebrews, so they waited 40 more years on earth for another tablet, one that would be indestructible, and which was buried in the desert instead. Earth, which is now too populated and polluted, was to be their future home. The takeover occurred prior to the appointed time of the return to earth. They need the tablet now more than ever to build a suitable infrastructure, and to revive a dormant and outdated industrial complex, or to enable them to terraform one of the other suitable planets they have since discovered. Although they have the advantage of knowledge and brainpower, they have not made much concrete progress in the past millenniums. You see, the thing is not only a data storage device; they had designed it to be a brain, which can evolve independently. Moreover, it can execute tasks and build any prototype. I am not entirely certain, professor Taggart, and it may just be intuition, but I believe that you were directed to the site by the alien himself. Perhaps he thought his chances with us were better than they would have been with the Chinese."

"I resent that," Taggart objected, "why, are we softer and easier to handle than the Chinese?"

"No, just you," professor Rhoades clarified.

"Ha, ha!"

"40 years; is that the time it takes them to travel to earth?" Lance inquired.

"That was then with the more limited propulsion system of that day's science; two days is the minimum now, give or take. Oh, I forgot to mention, they almost never die, so 40 years or 2 days does not affect much of anything. The sole concern is that the ruling dictatorship, which has been able to coerce the few scientists it had detained, is working night and day at finding a way to collapse the rebels' shield."

"Never die you say; what do they do with people like Pat Robertson, Wayne LaPierre, Quentin Tarantino, Bernie Madoff, Donald Trump, Rush Limbaugh, and the like?" Taggart asked.

He was relieved that he finally got a laugh.

"I'm glad you're back to being yourself, Mr. Spock, but what do we do now?" Tina wanted to know.

"We cannot very well give them something they might use against us, can we?" Mr. Rotcod interrupted, "I say finders keepers, don't you, professor Taggart?"

Before Taggart could possibly agree with Rotcod, Tina answered,

"I say we have no choice but give the thing back; they can come here any time they wish, and next time, angry and in numbers. I would not want to upset them."

"They would not do anything," Rotcod responded, "they never do, believe me. Besides you heard what the agent said, they do not believe in killing."

"Excuse me Sir!" Lance exclaimed, "You are saying that knowing they will not kill us should be our sole motivation? I am sure that short of exterminating us, a superior civilization such as theirs can think of many unpleasant ways to deal with juveniles like us."

At that point, Rotcod looked at his watch and excused himself,

"I am sorry, gentlemen… and lady, I have an appointment with the boss, but keep working, I'll see everyone in the morning, and please get some rest tonight. Professor Taggart, the tablet is yours if you would like to work on it later; Miss. Haley will assist you."

As the door closed behind him, Lance shook his head and whispered to Spock,

"What does he mean by they never do? ... I don't know about him!"

"I know!" Spock agreed.

Lance and Tina Sitting in a...

T he man was again at the telescope-like apparatus; he did not have to search, the now familiar look of the planet seemed affixed to the end of the tube.

"Come and see this," he said to the woman on the other side of the room.

"That's definitely our home, and right there in the center is the desert... and the Sinai," she said.

"Were you able to read the notebook? Make sure you memorize it for later," he told her.

"I think I got it, at least some of the equations and drawings. I could not find anything about the artifact," she informed him, "What do we do now?"

"Well... come here, let me show you," his voice lowered to a baritone.

"Oh, oh!" They thought simultaneously, "here we go again."

"Should we?" She asked demurely.

"I think we should be good guests and stay," he whispered.

They saw themselves reach for each other's hands; they felt their lips succumb to an attraction stronger than one between of a pair of binary stars, and then a viscous, pulsating want, the expectant and collective hunger of a thousand erotic dreams came lashing out at their unprotected and naked desire. They surged onto one another with deep, silent, quantum passion unrestrained by homebound inhibitions. The tidal effect of their mutual and suddenly unleashed magnetism sent them thrusting in turn one within the other. Every particle of her consciousness espoused one of his in a sweet, complete, and elemental bond. There was no urgency to reach that honey-laden summit; every instant of that moment was climactic, and every point of contact felt like the primary. It could not be a dream; it was at once earthly cognitive and paradise affirming. Every time, every place, every event must have led to this union. Every hope dashed or wish not granted could yield finally and eagerly to an aim greater than it had been: a validation for the big bang, an apple on the creator's desk. It had been fantasized about, written and sung about; there they were, discovering it, enveloped in it, and saturated by it. They were living it, actualizing it as it were.

Morning tiptoed to the windows to be first to see the smiles on their faces. Each looked in the direction of the other's room with dilating bliss still in their eyes, and perhaps at the same time blew kisses and whispered, "I love you." When she reached the conference room, he was already there alone; all senses on alert for the sound of her steps, the scent of her voluptuousness, the sight of her beauty, the feel of her touch, and the taste of her lips. As their hearts closed the distance between them, memories of the night before, emotions of the morning after broke through the fragile and bruised societal partition between them. Rendered utterly and singularly magnetized by the recent proximity to her Eden, he stood there, arms extended. Feeling perhaps for the first time emancipated from all of the world's conventions and free to love the love of her life, she allowed the moment to carry her, transport her, transform her, fill her, baptize her... She flew into the cradle of his arms, into a passion that surpassed anything she had ever heard about in all of her friends' grandiose tales of requited affections. The sound of ecstasy started to rise again, reverberating inside the newly uncovered chambers of their beings, reaching out to the walls of the room, threatening to set off the heat alarm, and... If only they could be alone, if only... what is that? How long had this person been knocking on the door? How many times did he knock before they heard him? Why did he knock? He must have seen them... could they care?

"Er... huh hum!" Well, it was Taggart!

They separated long enough to greet him with hugs and kisses,

"Morning Tag!"

"Good morning professor!"

"Wow, so much affection!" You two might want to let go of the hands and lips now," Taggart smirked. "I mean... you know... I love to see two lovebirds in the act of loving and all, but some people might want to start checking the surveillance tapes for secret night excursions; you know what I mean? Now that I mention it, I'm sure I heard some hushed footsteps in the hallway last night."

"You liar!" Tina pushed him away.

Phil staggered into the laughter-filled room with sleep tugging at his eyelids.

"What are you guys so happy about?" he moaned, "The world is on the brink..."

"It had better not be; some of us have loves to live, I mean lives to live," Taggart said with a wink at Lance and Tina. "My god, Phil, you look like you're about to fall down, did you sneak out to party or something?"

"I was in the War Room up until two hours ago; that makes three hours of sleep in two nights?" Phil answered. "Anyone has anything for me, because I have something for you!"

"We went back on our own last night, Lance and I, we made a few discoveries," Tina said, "When we go back to the W.R., you can fish out the details."

"Something else," Lance added, "I had a visit with Spock's old friend; he told me some things that will make it easier for them to decide on giving the artifact back, and to release the alien. He cannot stay here any longer, or his well-being will seriously be compromised. His idle physical body, as would be the case for ours, has physiological needs, and Earth sensitive life-support requirements."

"As far as the tablet is concerned," Taggart said, "since it has become such a national security issue, I withdraw my interest in it completely. I can now see why the university made it such a priority; the government was pressuring them. I understand that it is now more than an archeological piece. I want to go back to teaching, and to more mundane and less contentious projects that are not so risky to my health."

At that point, the door opened; Spock rushed in followed seconds later by a very attractive young woman. Her stern lab overcoat had a hard time trying to conceal her overly curvaceous figure. Phil feigned not noticing Taggart observing and awaiting a reaction or full-blown panting from him at the sight of her. Professor Rhoades almost made it home safely, but she turned to adjust the chair before sitting and dropped some files. Well, she had to pick them up, didn't she? He, Phil, had to exit in a hurry. He did. Taggart, knowing of Phil's propensity to self-combust when faced with extremely hot dishes, was choking with badly suppressed laughter. Meanwhile, she, the sultry one, kept her head down in her files, ostensibly oblivious to the professor's reaction to her... magnificence. Why then the vague attempt at concealing that mischievous smile?

"What happened?" Tina inquired, "Is he alright?"

"Probably went out for some cold water," Taggart smiled, "he hasn't been getting much... sleep; must have a lot on his... mind!"

"Forgive my late arrival," Spock interjected, "I was waiting for a call from the Chief, my boss. I may have to leave soon; I requested an audience with him to discuss the status of things. He will have to tell me why Mr. Rotcod has given orders that I could not leave the premises."

Professor Rhoades reentered, looking composed and insulated.

"I apologize," he cleared his throat, "must have been the A/C. Did I miss something?"

"I doubt it," Taggart smiled, "I think you got all of it."

She stood! Professor Rhoades was rocked again, but he kept his wits; he gave Taggart a look that said, "*See, I'm cool.*"

"My name is Ms. Roseanne Haley," she said, "please call me Roseanne. It is such a pleasure to have civilians around here; it makes some of us feel normal again. Personally, I would vote that we keep you here permanently, but I would just be selfish, wouldn't I! I am not previs to the agent's situation, but I am sure it is similar to that of the rest of you. Mr. Rotcod seems to think that it is best for everyone's safety that you remain here until the end of this crisis. He is convinced that the same people who abducted Ms. King, and broke into professor Taggart's office is out there hoping for another opportunity. He wants you to know that you do not have to worry about outside responsibilities; it is all covered. He has left me in charge... no, that is not correct; I am rather a liaison between you and him, and a guide to whatever you need while you are here. Mr. Rotcod had to meet the director last night; they have been in meetings with directors of several agencies. There is a briefing with the president, the defense secretary, the joint chiefs, and others going on as we speak. He will let us know of their decision as soon as the meeting is resolved. Professor Rhoades and professor Taggart, if you wish to resume your research, the War Room is staffed and ready. Please call on me for anything."

"Please call me Phil, I would like to feel normal as well," professor Rhoades said softly.

She smiled – oh, so very sweetly – unleashing the full might of her gorgeousness on his undernourished libido. The A/C... well, it malfunctioned again! She was merciless,

"Please, don't run away again!" she pounced.

"Please, catch me if I do!" he begged.

The two exited the conference room after some minutes with professor Rhoades carrying her files. Professor Taggart, who had been waiting outside with the others, approached and whispered in Phil's hear,

"If the A/C is cool, we need you for a little meeting in one of our rooms to discuss something."

"Whose room?"

"My room, ok?"

"Ok! I'll walk Miss Haley to her office and I'll join you in a minute."

"One minute, that's all?"

"Yes! Now get lost!"

The three walked to professor Taggart's room and everyone found a comfortable spot to slouch. The rooms were situated 200 feet from the offices via an L shape hallway. There was an abrupt impression of landing in a suburban Marriot hotel hallway from a Park Avenue office building. Outside the windows, there were plants with large and dark green leaves, and palms better suited for a California climate than an east coast environment.

"You guys notice something?" Tina said, looking out at the sunlit foliage, "the angle of the shadows has not changed since earlier."

"You're right," Taggart agreed, "You know what I think, it's artificial lighting; the earth did not stop turning, did it?"

"Definitely, those are tropical plants, they don't belong here," Lance added.

"Yeah, besides, we should be at least 3 or 4 levels below the surface. That is going to make it harder," Tina concluded.

"Should we let Spock know what we are planning, I mean, we can trust him, right?" Lance asked.

"I think so; what do you think? That's your expertise; do you think he is on our side? He is still a federal agent; he still has to answer to his boss," Taggart said.

"Where is Phil?" asked Tina, "we need to get started, only ten more hours to go before…"

The door opened, a smiling Phil tapped Taggart on the head and jumped on the bed next to Tina without saying a word, still grinning. All eyes turned in his direction.

"What?" he exclaimed, "Took too long?"

"Are you alright? Did she hurt you; did she touch you in any way?" Taggart asked him up closely and loudly.

"I was simply helping her back to her office with her stuff."

"I don't blame you; those are some real nice stuff she's got there!"

"Would you stop already?" Phil said as he tried to assume a serious demeanor, "Ok, what is the topic?"

While Tina was dying with laughter, Lance, not knowing that their friendship had endured and survived many such bouts of teasing and mockery, attempted to restore the peace by jumping in quickly with an answer.

"We are trying to decide whether we should include Spock in our plan."

"What is the plan?" professor Rhoades asked.

"We need to escape from this high tech dungeon," professor Taggart replied, "Although you may have found love, this isn't a two-way highway, you know. They will not let us leave now; we know too much."

"As I was telling you before," Lance again needlessly tried to intercede, "I was in contact with the alien last night; he is getting weak. He too needs rescuing, not only for his sake, but for the sake of humanity as well. If we don't let him go and complete his mission, they will come looking for him. Once they learn we have him captive or dead... well, who knows what the retaliation might be."

"You mean... whooooshhhh," Taggart made the sound and gesture of an annihilating explosion.

"Yes! I think he believes that's in the realm of possibilities," Lance replied.

"But they are a non violent species, aren't they?" Phil raised.

"Not all of them," Tina offered, "From what we understand, Lance and I, there are two distinct groups in the population of rebels; those who migrated in from the totalitarianism those millennia ago, and those born after. Those new additions often clash with the established order because it seems that nature, as it does here on earth, has a way of reclaiming its domain. They began to digress to their species' original, biological, mental, and psychological state."

"In psychology that's called regression, it's the process by which... So they are becoming more like we are, belligerent and distrustful," Professor Phil pointed out.

"In love that's call marriage," comedian Taggart pointed out.

"Thank you, professor!" Tina mocked, "So, how do we do it?"

"Well, this is where we need Spock, he's got the only inside track we know of, and I'm sure he can think of a way to get us out of here," Taggart said.

"You're forgetting something, Tag, Phil also has an inside track," Tina reminded him with a suggestive posture.

"Oh yeah, the hottie!" Taggart remembered, "Go boy, go do your thing with that Jerry Lewis/nutty professor act there. Try and stay up wind; that pheromone is a powerful A/C charmer; er... bring back Spock!"

Both Tina and Lance were doubled up with laughter. Phil stopped before opening the door, turned and sang,

"Lance and Tina sitting in a tree k-i-s-s-i-n-g."

That took Lance and Tina completely by surprise, because it was so unlike Phil. They froze and became red with embarrassment. As soon as the door closed, they turned toward Taggart and,

"It's your fault," Tina said.

"We didn't want him to know yet," Lance added.

"My fault," Taggart defended, "I didn't say a thing about it."

"You keep looking and winking at us, and making comments... 'Some of us have loves to live,' and all that," Tina complained.

"Oh, please!" Taggart protested, "You two are so obviously in love, I knew it the first time I saw you together in his office. That alien probably knows it. When he gets home, he'll write a book about the mating rituals of humans on planet earth; the title will be *Lance, Tina and a Tree.*"

Then he laughed and laughed, and looked up just in time to see two white and fluffy projectiles flying toward him.

Professor Phil's Ace in a Hole

"Thanks for joining us, agent Spock," professor Rhoades began, "let me start by saying that like you, we have an urgent need to get out of this place; unlike you, however, we have no means and no connection. Lance contacted the alien last night; he is hanging by a thread; if he goes, so does the human race. When they get here, he will better be alive and in possession of the artifact; he has to be rescued. We would like to be able to count on your help to accomplish those objectives, agent Spock. We realize that we are taking a risk by divulging our intentions to you, but it is our hope, agent, that your concern for the welfare of this planet has taken precedence over any contrived notion of loyalty to some government organization..."

"Hold it!" Spock abruptly interrupted, "do not belittle my allegiance to an organization whose mission is the welfare of this democracy, and this planet. And let me add by the way that you would not be able to do whatever you do without us, and men of other agencies like ours, doing what we do, including putting our lives on the line to safeguard a pristine environment for you to exercise your right to live the good life. So before you take the high ground, professor, and attempt to take me up there with you, remember that if I do anything to help you, I do it with the sanction of that very organization. While I have you here, professor, answer this for me, why do you, intellectual liberals, insist on believing that you are living on some moral island, unblemished by the results of others' actions, which you consider ruthless and unprincipled, and from which you benefit every day. You are not absolved simply by disapproving, nor are you redeemed by merely preaching dissent."

"You seem to know a lot about me, agent." professor Rhoades replied, "I must assume that you consider it your duty to investigate every American citizen who happens to stray within your considerable reach. I suppose my being this intellectual liberal is enough of a probable cause for you, as it was for Stalin, Mao, Pol Pot and his Khmer Rouge minions, Kim Jung-un, and others, like those morally bankrupt conservatives, for whom interest in education and human dignity is an anathema. I did not mean to touch a nerve, Sir; I apologize for having used the wrong words. Nevertheless, I thought it imperative to be reassured that we could count on your humanity, and not simply on your expertise. At the risk of sounding patronizing, and believe me I am not trying to be, agent, let me express my gratitude to you and to others of similar calling for what you do on our behalf every day, all over the world."

Spock was about to respond, instead he extended his hand in a gesture of conciliation. There was an uneasy stillness in the room as everyone avoided looking at anyone else. As would have been expected, Taggart broke the silence,

"Phew! I'm glad I'm not an intellectual; liberal or otherwise," he exhaled.

"Well then, I'll take your word for it and make sure to remove your name from my list of provocateurs," Spock promised.

The short burst of laughter that followed was more an expression of relief than a response to the humor in what was said by either of the two men. No one felt more relieved than Lance, who ventured,

"Agent Spock, is there any way you can help us break out of this place?"

"Correct me if I'm wrong," Spock responded, "but I was under the impression that you are here to accomplish a mission; you stayed willingly, did you not?"

"As I am sure that you are aware of the circumstances that prompted our arrival, the answer to that question is obvious," Phil countered, "the fact is you did not realized that your being sent here would result in your confinement as well. Someone wants you out of the way... wants us all out of the way."

"It would appear to be true," Spock conceded, "but if the chief is responsible to any degree for my confinement... or yours, someone must have convinced him that it is the safe and prudent thing to do given what we now know."

"Ok, so now what do we do?" Tina asked.

"I have been busy analyzing their security system;" Spock revealed, "I haven't been able to find a gap to exploit. However, if we can create some sort of internal crisis, a diversion if you will, I might be able to slip through undetected."

"Yes, what we're planning may be able to do just that," Phil claimed, "timing will be essential, however."

"Yes, Professor, you did mention that you had something for us. Is that what you've been working on all night?" Lance inquired.

"What have you got, Phil? Spit it out!" Taggart insisted.

"Well, I had the artifact in the War Room when I had a flash of genius; what if there were a way to make the machines and the artifact function as a unit. It is a machine in itself, albeit universes more advanced than anything we know. Instead of interpreting the language of dreams, our machine could talk to the hologram device, which in turn would become a blueprints-maker and a means of communication to convey our wishes to the artifact."

"Yeah, as Mr. Spock said, the artifact can manufacture things," Tina said, "if we can make it work... well, the sky is the limit, but I'm wondering whether its ability is confined only to the material and tangible."

"I see," Taggart exclaimed, "can it be asked to have a quality, or learn and display a talent; as a matter of fact, can it impart knowledge to humans?

"Well, I don't know..." Phil cautioned.

"Why not, professor? Can you tell us what were you able to achieve last night that exited you so much?" Lance inquired.

"I was able to wire the translator to the hologramer, and using the helmet, I was able direct the hologramer to execute a number of tasks. Then I asked myself, what if I integrated the artifact at the end of that chain, would it be possible with some creative adjustment to conjure up concrete, palpable, and functional objects."

"Like something that can travel through these walls," Lance said.

"Or make us invisible, or make us a Travel Light" added Spock.

"That's right," Tina added, "there's nothing thought or imagined that could not be accomplished. That's what you said, right? Well, after 3,000 plus years, nothing should be impossible to that thing."

"Let's do it then." Taggart bristled. "Wait a minute, how do we obtain the artifact and not the whole staff? Phil, it's time for your ace in the hole"

"You mean..."

"Yeah, that's her job; to assist us with what we need, right?"

"But she just refused to let me..."

"Or look at it this way, Professor;" Spock proposed, "you're an agent on a very crucial mission; its success hinges on you seducing the beautiful foreign socialite. But you're ambivalent; you've fallen in love with each other. You have a choice to make, love or country. What is it going to be, professor, love or humanity?"

"Personal experience?" Phil queried.

"More than once!" Spock admitted.

"Ok, you guys go to the War Room; give me a few," Phil barked.

Some fifteen minutes later, he returned to the group with Miss Haley. She was carrying a case tightly against her chest as if she would never let go of it.

"Roseanne?" Phil called with a palm raised.

Roseanne exhaled and then bit her bottom lip.

"Roseanne, please," he repeated softly, "we need to start now; you do understand, don't you?"

She slowly handed him the metal case, with a frown and a cringe, as if she were about to be given a shot with a giant syringe. As she let go, she whispered,

"You know he's going to kill me, don't you?"

"He's not going to kill you."

"Oh, you don't know him, this is his life. This is more important than anything or anyone."

"Then why don't you come with us?"

"I can't, I can't; this is my life too."

"If we don't succeed, there may not be a life for anyone after this."

Phil turned to the others, waiting patiently behind him, and began to yell out orders.

"OK, Lance, in the booth; Tina, go in there with him and help him with the helmet; Roseanne and I will make sure that all the connections are in place, then Tag and I will run to the hologram room. Now Lance, Tina, once you are done transmitting your directives, you'll have 20 seconds to disengage and be in that room before things are set in motion, so you'll have to haul ass. Got it?"

"What will those directives be?" Lance asked.

"I'll leave it up to you." Phil answered. "You know what we need. Better if you're spontaneous; the mind is able to convey more concise pictures that way."

Then addressing the whole room,

"Let's go!"

Everyone jumped into position without a word. Tina could not remember when she had seen Phil so assertive, and so much in command of a situation. Taggart was sure that the presence of sexy Roseanne had much to do with that. As the countdown reached ten, Phil turned, and to his surprised Spock was among them.

"What are you doing here?" he asked him, "You should be out there waiting for your cue."

"Hum... Changed my mind; this is as good an escape as any, isn't it?"

As the countdown reached two, Phil quickly opened the door and slid out before anyone could react or say a word. Two seconds later, there was a bright flash, brighter the light of many suns. The large pane of glass between the two rooms shattered, as an implosion brought the pieces flying inward toward the vacuum created by the group vanishing. Half a fraction of a second later, the small booth up front exploded with a reverse effect. Four balls of pure white light went past Phil and Roseanne and out of the doors, which came open as if by an invisible hand, and then it was pitch black. It took a few seconds for the emergency lights to activate. Phil and Roseanne instinctively followed, but by that time, it was too late for them to see only one ball of light dissolve into the ceiling, and continue on its way upward through concrete and steel, and toward sky and freedom.

Marilyn to the rescue

"Come here, check this out!"

"What?" the young man asked impatiently, as he slid away from his computer and toward Marilyn and the TV set.

"... What exactly did you see, officer?" asked the visibly exited reporter on the screen.

"I was coming down that exit right there when I saw four balls of light coming from that direction. They couldn't have been more than 200 feet in the air. They hovered for about ten... fifteen seconds, and then three of them merged into one and went northwest; the other changed direction and went south. Those people... they all saw it; it's a miracle there wasn't a pile-up."

"How big would you say they were?"

"If I had to take a guess, I'd say no bigger than twelve to fifteen feet across each."

At that point, Chris grabbed the remote and turned off the set.

"What did you do that for? You know that's rude, right?" Marilyn yelled.

"You came here to do some work, right? Well, do it or..."

"Or what? You'll throw me out?

"Listen Marilyn, if you want to waist your time with that crap and what's his name, be my guest; I deal with real life, know what I'm saying?"

"His name is Lance... and it's not crap; you'll see for yourself some day."

"Yeah, yeah, whatever... why don't you go get us some Micky Dees; 20 enough? You know what I want."

She snatched the $20 bill from him, turned around, and froze on the spot. Seconds elapsed before she could regain command of her physical functions. She tapped Chris on the back a few times without uttering a word.

"Come on man, go already. Stop messing around, this is important; I don't have time to fool around right now."

"Look!" Marilyn was finally able to say.

He turned around, and almost fell over his equipment.

"What the... get the hell out of my place, man. I don't care who or what you are," Chris groaned, while reaching for the baseball bat that he always kept nearby.

"Oh my god, they're coming!"

"What?"

"Wait!" Marilyn intervened, "This one is trying to say something; oh my god, it's Lance!"

The almost contour-less lights crossed the long empty floor of the loft. As they approached, they consolidated into Lance, Tina, and Taggart.

"What in hell are you, man; a nightmare from your dream experiments?" Chris barked as he tried to keep from showing his panic.

"Can we sit" Lance asked, "we've been flying all night and our..."

"Your wings are killing, yeah... Answer me, what are you and what are you doing here? You know you're not welcome..."

"Look at us, man; don't tell me you're not impressed," said Lance, "I had to share this with you, bro. we're on an adventure more fantastic than we could have ever imagined. I want you to be part of this; forget about our past differences. This is bigger than anything we've done together, this is something that the CIA, FBI, the Chinese, the Russians, and every other government on earth would like to get their hands on."

"So you think coming here with your little demonstration of magic, and speech of forgive and forget would make up for what you've done?" Chris asked, then turning to the others, "I hope the rest of you realize what a poser this guy is. Oh, I know, he's just another poor young man from the hood who's found his way after many wasted years full of bad deeds. I fell for it too, man; we were tight, two unlikely brothers with similar dreams and ideals who would do anything for one another, friends to the end and all that. Until one day, he got tired of the hood, Marilyn, and me; we had served his purpose. So, he called his rich dad for help and forgiveness, and promised to go back to school, and to the more... civilized white-bread-life he once knew; the one he was beginning to crave for. He abandoned me in the middle of an important project we were both working on. I begged him to stay until we complete something that he knew was key for our business, but he'd made up his mind that he'd reached his stop. Time to get off this train; hasta la vista, baby."

"Come on, Chris, it wasn't like that at all," Lance defended," we talked about it way before I actually left, before I even thought about calling home. But you refused to understand that I never had any intention of staying in one place for good; I wanted to be a good partner and a friend while I was here and after I left, but that was all."

"You know what, I don't need any friend," Chris countered, "you and your magicians' troupe can get the hell out. I'd like to say that it was good to see you, but..."

"Wait a minute! So much testosterone," Marilyn jumped in, "you guys used to be best buds; everyone has the right to pursue his own dream, or change the course of his life, right? It's a free country, isn't it? He thinks he's found the biggest thing in his life, and he wants to share it with you, his friend; won't you at least listen?"

"Still defending him..." Chris shook his head, "he ran out on you too, Marilyn, but you went after him, followed him to that college of his. You still love him, don't you? You still expect he'll notice and make you his woman some day. Wake up, Marilyn, he's not one of us, he's..."

"Shut up," Marilyn punched him in the chest, "you're so stupid; think you know everything, huh! You wanna know the truth, you're the one that I always... But I was just a friend; just one of the guys. Haven't you noticed? I'm the only one still around. You drove them all away with your coldness and your obsession with this high-tech stuff. At first, I tried to use him to make you jealous, but I found out that he's a real nice guy; sorry Lance. But it's you, Chris, still... guess I'm the stupid one."

There was silence as Lance and Chris glanced sideways at each other.

"Who are those guys creeping around out there?" wondered Tina, looking at the monitor near the ceiling.

"You brought Five-O to my crib, man?" Chris shrieked.

"No dude, this is not the police, they're feds." Lance explained.

"Oh, they're feds; thank God they have no power and no jurisdiction in this American city; I feel better. What have you gotten me involved in, Lance?"

"They have no interest in you, relax! They're like your typical Men in Black types. That's what I was saying, Chris, they know what we got, and they want it. They know we're here; come with us now before they set up their trap or..."

"I'm not going anywhere, I ain't done nothing. You broke into my place; that's all I know."

"Hey guys, they're coming in," Tina warned.

"It means the trap is already set, hear that helicopter?" professor Taggart asked, "What do we do? Do you have a secret exit somewhere?"

"Where do you think you are, man?" Chris answered.

"We can be invisible," Tina reminded them," why don't we just..."

"No, it won't work," said Lance, "They have this electromagnetism-based device that can detect any living entity."

"I know... why don't you hide in cyber space;" Marilyn beamed, "if you can be light, you can be other energies, can't you?

"Wow, Marilyn, what an idea!" Chris kissed her on the cheek, then turning to the others, "you guys can do that, can you?

"Yes, we can, set us up; I'll tell you what, find any non-military aircraft production site," Lance answered," we cannot keep traveling as we have been; we need the protection of an insulating vehicle."

Chris sat in front of his computer and searched frantically for an access conduit. Meanwhile, the commotion outside was getting more perceptible, as the agents broke down the multiple reinforced entry doors one after another.

"Go, go," shouted Chris, as he triumphantly turned toward Lance, Taggart, and Tina, who had already metamorphosised into their glowing alter-egos."

"*We'll see you guys again*," Tina projected.

They merged into one form, and then streamed into the screen, and into cyber space. As some residual light began to fade, and the room returned to its gloomier appearance, the final door fell. Men – not all in black – poured into the loft; armed with all sorts of electronic sniffers, and other strange weaponry, they began to search every inch of the floor, ceiling, crawl spaces, closets, bathrooms, and sinks. Not even the cat could avoid scrutiny; it was thoroughly wan-screened. Chris stood there in awe at the array of electronic devices, while Marilyn protested vehemently.

"What do you think you're doing?" she demanded, "Do you have a warrant? Do you have probable cause or something? You have no reason to be here. Who are you people?"

"Yeah, who are you?" echoed Chris, "I'm just a struggling entrepreneur, and this is my home and place of business, There is nothing illegal going on here."

"Yeah, yeah," mocked Mr. Rotcod, "we all know what you do, Chris. Somebody has been keeping an eye on you since your little foray into one of the most sensitive Government facilities, but don't worry, we have bigger fish to fry. We are willing to forgive and forget if you help us. We know that your former partner is here with his friends; they are in serious trouble, and you may be an accessory. Now, where are they?"

"I don't know what you're talking about, man; nobody else is here, unless he's invisible or something," Chris snickered."

"Oh, you think it's funny," Rotcod approached menacingly, "well, we're going to have to..."

"Listen to this, gentlemen," one young agent motioned to the rest to pay attention to the television set in the corner, "the internet has blacked out, it's panic out there..."

"I see... so tell me, Chris, why are you able to have access?" Rotcod grinned.

"Look at this, Sir," said the nerdy looking agent who for a while had been studying a kind of convoluted old pack-man configuration on Chris' computer screen, "I think it's him... it's them, they have high-jacked the internet, they're headed toward something; see, that's a deliberate path."

"Where are they going?" Rotcod asked Chris, "A government facility I guess, that's right up your alley, isn't it."

"Give me a second, Sir, I think I can find out," said the agent at Chris' computer. After a few seconds, he announced, "their destination may be the Longview Aircraft Company."

"Figures... well, come on, let's go... we'll see you later, Chris," Rotcod seethed, "Zoids, you stay here and keep them company, let us know if anything changes. You will be a good host, wont you, Chris?"

"Zoids? Your name is Zoids?" Marilyn asked as soon as Rotcod and his little army had departed.

"That's my street name, my alias kind of. I've always been good with a computer. At an early age five I think, I so impressed my father that he got me my own grown-up computer. He wanted to be able to have access to his without me in the way all the time. In school and in the street, I was Freakazoid, which morphed into Zoids somehow."

"How did you get into spying on Americans citizens?" Chris inquired.

"I met some really bad dudes in college; their expertise was getting into top secret areas. Anyway, I was caught hacking into very sensitive government domain. By then I was eighteen; they gave me a choice, serve or go to jail, so I took the oath. I heard a lot about you, Chris; you were my role model. Dude, you've done some things!"

"That was then; I'm just a businessman now."

"Oh sure, sure; me too," Zoids smiled.

To Build a UFO

There was a mini explosion as they exited the cyber highway. One of the monitors in the plant security center shattered. The three operators, who had been at the controls, stood frozen with fear at the emergence of a big ball of light. When the luminous apparition divided into three separate glowing humanoids, it was too much; they bolted out of the room and sounded the alarm. Armed security men arrived to see the three gleaming beings exit the monitoring room. They pulled out their weapons and waited for an order. When none was immediately given, and shaky hands gained their own volition, the weapons began firing while the men backed away. The radiant figures continued to approach unfazed. But as armed men are wired to do, they continued shooting until one of them panicked, and then it was a stampede to get out of there.

"What do we do now?" asked Taggart.

"He needs to be in that hangar over there," Lance revealed.

"He, who's he?" Tina asked.

"The brain, the artifact; we need proper transportation. He's a builder, remember?" Lance reminded, "Just walk straight ahead, we cannot be hurt as long as we have on this shield."

They made it across the wide path that separated two rows of giant hangars, to the sound of automatic weapons, and tear gas erupting all around. They reached the four story high doorway and ducked to the left behind a small booth where they look frantically for the switch that activated the giant door. Outside, the throng of uniformed men and plain-clothed agents approached cautiously through the fading fog. Twenty feet from the entrance, the gas masks wearing mob parted to allow an eight-foot tall android to stump his way to the front where he remained motionless for a moment. He scanned the structure with a wide turn of his head from shoulder to shoulder, as if he could see through solid walls; as if formulating a course of action. Inside, the three had gathered in the small booth. Lance having collected everyone else's luminous alter-element, which he consolidated into his own, exited the small hiding place and floated across the floor to the strange-looking craft at the center of the huge hangar. It was a prototype of some sort. It did not look like any commercial or military airplane that anyone had ever seen. It had been rumored, due to the extreme isolation, the high-level clearance required for admittance, and very extensive security measures displayed for a mile outside the area, that the Longview Aircraft Company was more of a military supplier than a public concern. That unconventional looking ship was enough to convince Lance who then realized why Mr. Artifact had chosen to bring them there; he was the influence behind Chris making that choice.

As he stepped inside the forward half of the still unassembled craft, the artifact left his body, and permeated the control panel. At that moment, the vehicle began to vibrate and purr. The sound of an army of ants moving in all direction inside the hull followed. In a minute, it was all over. As if complying with some unheard order, Lance turned toward the open door and called for the others to join him. Tina and Taggart could not believe the scene before their eyes. Wires went from every inch of the vessel to the walls, ceiling, floor, and every object inside the hangar, forming a giant web through which they had to navigate to find their way to the craft. As soon as they entered, the two halves came together and the purring resumed. They began to observe something fantastic; all around them, there was a fluid transformation to a silver-non-descript and even surface, interrupted only by a circular table-like configuration in the middle of the floor, and a bench partitioned for many, on which helmets and gloves awaited. They were now standing in a circular room, 30 feet in diameter; no windows or doors were noticeable. They stood there mesmerized by it all. When the building artifact had completed its shape-shifting work, Lance turned to Taggart and Tina and asked them to wear the helmets and gloves. When they did, the visor revealed a receded floating panel with schematics offering a layout of controls and dials undetectable to the naked eye.

"Ok now, with your right index finger, touch the red circle at its twelve o'clock spot," Lance directed.

They did, and wherever they looked, the walls, the ceiling, and the floor, in turn, gained a localized transparency that allowed them to view the world outside the craft.

"...to go back to standard, touch the center; we'll learn about the rest later, now we have to take off," Lance announced.

"We are still inside, aren't we?" Tina wondered.

"I guess we should know by now that 'It' works in mysterious ways," Taggart reasoned.

"Activate your visor again," lance suggested.

As the circular side panel became a series of windows, they realized that they had already left the hangar through the round hole in the center of the roof; the Longview Aircraft Co. was now 1,000 feet below them. The next moment, they observed the structure crumbling, and a cloud of dust rising where it had been.

"Gee, what happened?" Taggart wondered, "Hey Lance, perhaps you should have been gentler."

"Well, we had to borrow some construction material to build our... UFO, that left the building practically hollow and fragile; that big robot and his laser didn't help either," Lance explained.

"So that's what the artifact was using those tentacles for; to suck elements from the surroundings," Tina concluded.

"And synthesized them into a sort of quasi-living substance with cognitive properties," Lance added.

"This is something!" Taggart exhaled, "if you had told me of the possibility of such a thing yesterday, I would have advised therapy. Man, this is..."

"Well," Tina bristled, "you would have sounded like one of those scientists who demand evidence and corroboration by some empirical scientific convention every time somebody makes a claim outside of what has been accepted by them. Where would we be had Copernicus, Galileo, Newton, Einstein, and so many others subscribed to that kind of short mindedness?"

"Whoa! Perhaps, I should advise therapy," Taggart reacted, "do I detect a lot of rage in that tirade, T? I'm not used to seeing you take it so..."

"Hey guys, we are being followed," Lance informed.

"Must be Rotcod; what do we do?" Taggart asked.

"Turn on your visor. It's the air force, a couple of F-22s. Don't you worry, Artie knows what to do," Lance replied.

"Artie?" Taggart queried.

"Artie, the artifact," Lance clarified.

"Really... you hear that, T., you have competition, I think."

"I'm not worried, there's not enough Viagra in the world."

"Don't forget, Artie works in mysterious ways."

"Yes, but Artie is not from Venus, if you know what I mean."

"Well, he's not from Mars; we know that."

"He is from Cronart," Lance interjected, "that's what he's telling me."

"That's right," Tina added, "we saw it in that space grid from the manual in the observation room. It had a line going from a planet designated Cronart to our planetary system. Why do I know that? It was not in English."

"Yeah? I didn't notice it; Artie just told me," Lance admitted, "great catch."

"Ok, now what?" Taggart asked.

"We're going to Langley to get Spock and the alien," Lance announced.

They flipped down their visors in time to see a blur, and then Langley was beneath them.

Quarantined

"Pick up the phone, Marilyn... please," Chris requested.

"What phone?

"You can't hear the phone ring?"

"You're ok?

"Yes I'm ok," Chris answered impatiently, "stop looking at me like that; there's a phone..."

"Calm down, Chris, it's me, Lance; this is one of our new apps. We can communicate without any physical equipment, kinda like ESP; the ring was just for effect."

"Man! You just scared the hell out of Marilyn; she thought I was going crazy," Chris exhaled, "you mean you can be inside my head any time you want?"

"I cannot hear what you're thinking, if that's what you mean; I can only communicate my thoughts to you. You see, we all operate along our own individual frequency so to speak, and Artie, that's the source of our power, has the ability to identify and store it the moment he meets someone... Is everything all right? We're going to rescue a friend, and

then we'll stop by to get you guys, if you've changed your mind about coming along."

"I might as well! Thanks to you, I can't be here anymore. I'm sure that guy is coming back; it's my butt now that he can't get his hands on you."

"I figured that... Cool! We'll see you in a while then..."

"Wait! Is that you everybody's talking about in the news?" There is a UFO being chased by jetfighters all over Jersey. Everybody's out in the street watching, but they have this guy in Washington saying it's Homeland Security conducting exercise maneuvers or something, but I had a feeling it might be you guys. How did you... never mind... so I'll expect you to beam me up or something?"

"Something like that."

"So he changed his mind? Tina inquired.

"Yeah, he'll come," Lance smiled.

"Hey guys," Taggart called "I've been able to access the local media; it seems that Washington DC is under quarantine. No one can enter or leave the city, neither by land nor by air. They're not saying why, other than that it is for the good of the public."

"They must already be here," Lance said, "the ship from Cronart is over Washington; they have the city covered with an invisible, impenetrable shield. Remember the ultimatum, 'it'll remain that way until the alien is released.'"

"Ok... let's go get him then," Taggart directed, "but be aware of traps; Rotcod could be down there."

The trio slid down a tube of light that continued on to the lower basement of the building, and then horizontally toward the chief's office. Although they were able to perceive the contrasting hues of metals, cement, and other building materials, there was no sensation of friction; no olfactory or auditory impressions were acquired. They shined out of the wall, passing through the near transparent substance that it became. As they solidified into their earthly human forms, the door flung open violently.

"What is... oh... er, Craig, I believe your friends are here," the Chief called.

"My friends... they are?" Spock exclaimed as he squeezed by the Chief, "That's what I was trying to explain, Chief, they will corroborate my story."

"We have to go! Where is he?" Taggart asked.

"They're here, over Washington as we speak, agent Spock." Tina added, "We must return him now or..."

"I am sorry;" the Chief spoke, "I've let Rotcod convince me that it would better serve national security if he had custody of him. We were on our way to see him."

"You will not find him," Lance said, "he is on a plane headed for the mountain."

"You mean..." Tina started.

"Yes," Lance responded, "he is going to find the alien's craft; Artie believes that Rotcod may have been able to torture him into revealing the ship hiding spot in the mountain."

"That miserable, misleading son of a..." The chief groaned, "He must be carrying out his own agenda; he hasn't changed since... We have to beat him to it."

"Not to worry," Lance declared, "everybody, huddle up."

As they did, they become one ball of light vanishing into the wall, and the next instant, they were sliding up Artie's photons tube to the craft above.

"My God!" the chief exclaimed, "Craig, I'm sorry I doubted you, it's true... this is real; who's piloting this thing?"

"The artifact, Sir," Lance replied, "It is almost a living, thinking computer with task-performing capabilities, like building this ship; we call him Artie."

"Ok... well then, tell Artie what the plan is; where we want to go." The chief directed.

"He knows," Taggart responded, look, there he is; see that plane over there? Oh, you cannot… put on a helmet, sir."

"How did we… he must have left over an hour ago," marveled the Chief, who became able to see out of the otherwise invisible windows.

"We can travel at almost unlimited speed," Taggart explained, "and we are invisible to them; they can see us only if we let them."

"Can I speak to Rotcod?" The Chief asked.

"Go ahead." Lance said.

"Oh… it's you guys!" a suddenly materialized figure exclaimed, "Len, what are you doing… so you're with them now?"

"You don't seem too surprised, Les." The Chief remarked.

"What do you think I do, Len? My people are quite acquainted with those creatures. We've seen them come and go, but I think this one is the spearhead to a more permanent move; and you're helping them, along with these idiots. We're supposed to be the first and last lines of defense, for Pete's sakes; you'd rather capitulate without a fight?"

"Les listen, there is no conflict, there is no invasion, and if there were, we would be powerless against them. All we have to do is return the artifact and the alien, and they'll go away. I went along with your scheme because I was not told all there was to know. You misrepresented the situation, as well as what I believe to be your personal agenda in this."

"I don't know about you, but I am doing what I was sworn to do." Rotcod countered, "I took an oath to defend this nation against all invaders, regardless of origin or superiority. We have an extraordinary chance here, Len; we can leapfrog millenniums of human evolution with one smart act. We retain possession of the artifact and we'll be so far ahead of those ET's that they'll think twice about coming here uninvited ever again. Look what you have built with that thing! Now, what are you going to do, give it back? No! I say finders keepers; this is our planet. We are not some kind of free storage warehouse. Perhaps we should ask for a claim ticket; how do we even know that it really belongs to these particular aliens?"

"Let me understand," Tina interjected, "you see a chance to advance human evolution by millenniums? Well, it seems to me, sir, that even if it were possible to have that level of knowledge at our disposition, the potential capacity of the human brain in its present state would not be able to accommodate it. Evolution is more than knowledge; it is everything that distances us from our animal essence, and brings us closer to our ideals, and to our higher non-physical self. There is a school of thought that our species was bio-engineered from primate to homosapien; if that is true, the resulting evolution if you will, apart from the way we are better able to navigate on the survival plane, has proven to be miniscule. With all our science and technology, we have not changed very much. What I am trying to say, sir, is that you cannot trust humankind with that much power. It would be tantamount to letting a six year old play with your AK47; bad things will happen to his brother, or to you."

"Well," Rotcod responded, "I can see that it's a waste of time trying to reason with a bunch of blind idealists, so I'm going to spell it out for you: you cannot have him, and if you try to by force, he'll fry; he will be in a state wherein connection with his body is irreversibly severed. By the way, the longer you keep me here, the more you put him at risk. Len, you know me; I do not bluff."

"Yes, I know you," the chief scoffed.

"We are going to send you back to your craft, Mr. Rotcod," Lance said, "but you will still be under our control. We will land on an island to make the exchange. Once we verify that we indeed have the entity in question and that he is in good shape, we will let you leave with the artifact. Is that to your convenience, sir?"

"Yes it is," Rotcod replied, "but I am warning you, no deception and no tricks. We are not completely toothless, I assure you; even with our last breath we can inflict a pretty serious bite."

"Not to worry, sir, our only concern is the welfare of the alien," Tina said.

"Hey Les, try not to display too much of yourself on this," the chief added; "we see you trying to deviate from our agreement even a little, and we will let them take you back home with them. I'm sure they would like some payback for their friend's abduction."

Rotcod turned to stare at him with contempt, and then in a flash he was gone.

Time and Seek

"Ok guys, what is the plan?" the chief inquired, "We're not really going to hand him over the artifact, are we?"

"Well, we have no choice." Lance answered, "I believe that maniac would not hesitate harming the alien. We'll give it to him all right; I don't think he'll like it though. Artie has a plan."

"Where is that island?" Taggart asked, "I hope there is a nice sandy beach; I'm going to need some R&R after this."

"Oh yeah, there's a beach," Lance told him, "great accommodations, but it's all self-service; we'll be the only ones there."

"The only ones?" Tina questioned.

"Wait!" the chief exclaimed, "Are we going to land on that radiation contaminated island that was accidentally nuked back in seventy three?"

"Well... yes..." Lance admitted.

"Ok, hum... you guys don't need me;" Taggart reasoned, "I think I'll get off now, thank you very much. We have any parachutes in this thing?"

"Don't worry, Artie will neutralize the radiation; it'll be completely safe when we land," Lance reassured everyone, "we need to be in a place no one else wants to be."

"I see… we don't want any witnesses in case we have to get tough with what's his name," Taggart surmised.

"Mr. Alien will not exactly be thrilled about his captivity." Spock cautioned, "Should we be concerned about possible retaliation?"

"Well, that's where you come in, agent Spock," Lance said, "Artie's plan involves you rejoining the alien. Your physical person will insulate him from any adverse action Rotcod may initiate, and at the same time, you may be able to defuse any retaliatory disposition on his part. Artie has been able to analyze the mechanism; you and the alien will have to figure out which side of the trap is the exit side. You can enter on either side, but with him there's only one way to exit."

"Is it wise to put the agent in such a vulnerable position?" the chief worried, "I mean, last time it did not play out too well for him."

"Begging your pardon, sir, last time Artie was not at the planning stage," Taggart offered.

"We'll be in the driver's seat this time around," Lance promised.

"You understand that he will be privy to our plans and intentions the moment I link with him; he will know everything I know," Spock cautioned.

"If you accept this mission, agent, Artie will edit your memory file to exclude anything that may compromise a conflict-free association with us. It will be reinstated upon your return to being a single unit," Lance revealed.

"I imagine, agent Spock, that there may be an insidious kind of process that comes into play when two entities share the same body; one has to yield to the other." Tina reasoned, "So stay on your guards. Keep reminding yourself of the mission; don't get pulled too far into his gravitational zone, so to speak."

"I understand…" Spock replied, "Ok, then when do I go, and when do I make my escape?"

"Well…" Lance paused, "we'll have to wait for him and the pilot to exit because we don't want him to be aware of our subterfuge, and then you will be beamed into position. Once you're there, you, with the alien, will be able to simply walk out of the trap and out of the plane."

"And… Craig, be careful with that snake," the chief warned, "he can be quite unpredictable," Then tuning to the others, "Can we arrange a diversion of some sort? That could also be his cue to exit before Rotcod can set off any back-up contingency that he surely will have planned."

"I'm sure Artie can do something;" lance assured him, "he will communicate it to him at that time. Ok, agent?"

"Oh… one more thing, try and keep your own complexion this time, agent; we like you better this way," Taggart advised.

"I have a friend in the beauty supply business," Tina revealed, "perhaps we can convince him to transport back a load of skin cream and stuff. With the right marketing strategy, those Cronart ladies might develop a taste for a little pink on their cheeks."

"Yeah," Spock responded, "I can see the opening up of a new interstellar trade route; earth products and crafts going one way, high tech appliances coming back. I'll try and get him interested, but I don't think he needs the money."

"He doesn't," Lance offered, "I think he was the rich man in a grand mansion that I saw in a dream."

"Oh yeah… that was you, wasn't it;" Spock realized, "I did think that my nephew was acting strange that evening. Wow… that was my old place before the exodus."

"Your nephew… your place?" Taggart questioned.

"You know… his nephew, his place; I'm still adjusting. It's been a while with him at the helm," Spock explained, "he more than likely was the young man whose skills you later used to fight that gang in your dream."

"Hey, we're not moving anymore," Taggart said, having donned his helmet.

"Well, we're here; give Artie a minute to clean up a bit, and then we'll know what the plan is," Lance said.

"What the... what are those things? Hey guys, take a look outside, I believe we're surrounded," Taggart sounded the alarm.

What Taggart was seeing was a formation of unusually shaped crafts deployed around them. The noticeably hostile vehicles circled slowly and methodically, and then after a few more revolutions, they started to shoot balls of light from protrusions in their undersides.

"I don't think they are USAF or anyone else's we know," Spock said.

"Are we under attack, are they shooting at us?" Tina wondered.

"Must be a type of laser cannon," the chief surmised.

"Lance, what's going on?" Taggart asked.

"Artie did not want to alarm us," Lance obliged, "but he knew that Rotcod's plane was being tracked by something that he had not been able to identify until now. We can safely assume they're Rotcod's allies."

"Must be what he meant by his last bite," Spock said.

"Until this episode, I thought OSID was just a product of someone's obsession with ET's," the chief remarked, "well, I guess they not only have been here all along, we've partnered with them."

"And you are, sir, the director of the foremost intelligence body in the world," Tina commented, "Well, if it is of any comfort, I hear that the president is kept out of the loop as well."

"Rotcod doesn't want to be just a partner; he wants to be the CEO. He said they never do anything, well, these guys sure are trying pretty hard," Taggart remarked.

"We must be enclosed in some kind of a shield. How long can it withstand this? We're getting pummeled!" the chief worried.

"Well, we are not able to use our speed to escape because that airbus out there would be torn apart, and we can't let it loose. I think that's what they're trying to induce us to do, and then Rotcod would be free to proceed with his agenda. Wait... Artie is analyzing their structure... he is... oh my god, that's amazing! He's absorbing and incorporating their technology on the fly. It's remote reverse-engineering... man!"

"He had better hurry; it looks as if they're preparing for a new assault," the chief warned.

"Yeah, they sure are; they're in a vertical loop now. They're just a blur." Spock added.

"Ok, we got it! We cannot move in space, so we'll move another way; we're going to play a game of time and seek. It's just like hide and seek; only they have to figure out not where but when we are."

"Looks as if they're getting reinforcement," Tina worried, "wait... there are swastikas on those planes; it's the Luftwaffe!"

"It's working!" Lance celebrated, "That's ok; they can't hurt us. We've been transported to 1943; now let's see whether... oops, Artie say they're coming; they've found us."

"They can match our every move; how are we going to escape them?" The chief inquired.

"Ok, we're going to see some quick changes of venue," Lance announced, "that'll give Artie some leeway to plan our next course of action... Wow, that was fast! Ok, Artie thinks he can use the tactic of countermeasures to confound them. You all remember the Roadrunner accelerating in multiple directions at once. Ok, as soon as they make contact again, we'll send a countermeasure or false target with our definite characteristics in each of ten points in time and hope that they won't bite on the right one for a while. If by chance they seek us out, we have one more trick up our sleeve: the fake door. Ok, here we go!"

"Where, I mean when are we, Lance?" Tina asked, "It looks like virgin landscape down there."

"We are in the fifteen century, Leonardo Da Vinci's time," Lance replied, "too bad we can't stop and visit. Artie is working on a definite strategy to give us time to return to our mission, which we cannot complete with those guys around, pestering us. He wants us to stay calm whatever we see or don't see, and to be ready for an experience unlike anything our sense of reality could ever enable us to imagine."

"Wish Phil was here; he would really be intrigued by all this," Tina sighed.

"Well, she was intriguing, wasn't she? Wherever he is, I hope it was worth him staying behind. Hopefully Rotcod has not made him and Roseanne pay for him being outsmarted," Taggart said.

"She is his niece, the poor girl; it's the only world she knows. She is a well-trained scientist and a very capable administrator; she practically runs that agency for him. You know, I'm really leaning toward offering Rotcod to the alien for re-education, it might appease him to have his captor at his mercy; Rotcod tricked me into doing it." the chief lamented.

"Then he can turn him over to the other side; I'm sure he'll be more receptive to their views," Spock suggested.

"Ok... hum, I am going to try and convey Artie's plan to you, but it's very technical and mysterious... er, perhaps Miss King can do a better job at it. Artie is going to download it onto you, Miss King," Lance announced.

Miss King's now suddenly erect body shuddered, her eyes closed and then slowly reopened, unfocussed and wide. After a few seconds, she came out of her catatonic state and uttered a,

"Phew... what a charge! Gentlemen, what Artie has just downloaded into my brain had to be filtered through my limited ability to understand scientific ideas far beyond our most purely conceptual hypotheses. I'll call on my basic knowledge of quantum physics to translate what I understand. See, some of the things that we are just now beginning to think about scientifically have been known facts to these guys for millenniums. Their arrested development, due to the religious takeover, has made concrete application of their science near impossible. However, Artie here has been busy advancing and applying it. This vehicle, which is not only a spacecraft but also a very advanced laboratory, is a testament to that."

"Excuse me, Miss King," Lance interrupted, "Artie wants me to communicate this to you; he has already started the process of leading our pursuers to the fake door. We are not at the moment what we seem to be; we are merely what we remember to have been before the transformation. Because we've been concentrating on Miss King's words, we have not had time to be self-aware, but don't be alarmed if things or people appear strange to you just by you thinking about them in a particular way. You, however, will know who and what is. Go ahead, Miss King."

"Thank you Lance," Tina continued, "before I go any further, I would like to say this, time and space are irrelevant at this juncture. All of this is happening instantaneously and in a dimension, if you will, where matter as we know it is non-essential to existence and time is... well, static. A more obscure offshoot of the theory of time dilation, which is mathematically confirmed, proposed that if you can dilate a second to near infinity, whether by using high velocity or gravity, a particle could be in so many places that it is relatively everywhere at once. It is a super particle with the omnipresent ability to be an atom, or all atoms, all electrons, all molecules, all cells, all trees, all planets and so forth. Furthermore, the argument among quantum field theories physicists on whether space-time and internal symmetries are combinable has long been resolved by our Cronartians; the answer is yes. The Travel Light is a product of that science. The fact is we have navigated that world all day; we have been alternately particles and waves, matter and energy, atoms and photons. Artie has used that science to conjure up a... I'd call it a quantum version of us that can be substituted at the right juncture. Artie has provided our pursuers with a tunnel, as it were, to make it possible for them to follow us. Because the two versions of us cannot dwell in the same dimension, the appearance of that very real and foolproof countermeasure will automatically catapult us back to our own reality, as they unsuspectingly continue to pursue it to the fake door. Once they go through it, they will find, courtesy of Artie's slight of hand, what they'll think at first is our universe, and... well, good luck finding an exit!"

"That is truly extraordinary and far reaching," the chief exhaled, "it brings to mind what you told Rotcod on humankind not being able to handle that kind of power. I hate to sound like him, but how do we know that our soon to be alien friends are at the developmental level to harbor such a thing responsibly?"

"We don't; well, we hope... besides what choice do we have?" Tina asked.

"I know one thing; probably no one in the galaxy would be safe with it in our possession. We'll have a new Christopher Columbus discovering new planets, new worlds, warring, conquering, plundering, enslaving, segregating, exterminating, and spreading the gospel of earthling supremacy; you know... the good old days that our conservative friends on the right are so nostalgic for," Taggart mocked.

"Ok, we're back! Let's prepare to go down there and..." Lance started.

"Hey... er, what just happened?" Taggart queried.

"Yeah, strange," Spock agreed, "it all felt normal while we were wherever we were, but now I don't seem to remember a physical context. I do remember being and talking with all of you, but..."

"Like a dream where the surrounding is vague, but you go on as in real life?" Lance asked.

"Yeah..."

"It was real, gentlemen; whatever the perspective we had individually, it was what we each needed for a working reality. But we were there; it all happened," Tina explained.

"No change in the plan," Lance informed, "we will set Rotcod's plane down first, and then Artie will transport agent Spock in position the minute they walk out."

"How can we be sure they'll exit before we're in position ourselves?" the chief asked.

"Artie will make it the likely course of action for them," lance replied, "sir, if you don't mind, you will stay here for now, your presence may antagonize him; agent Spock, you will wait for Artie to determine the right moment for you to go. Miss King, professor; are we ready?"

"Wow... déjà vu!" Taggart exclaimed, "I've live this moment before. No, it was Phil, but the motivation is the same."

"Oh, be quiet!" Tina elbowed him.

Déjà vu

They zipped down on a plateau, where vestiges of buildings foundations and charred stumps indicated that a kind of cataclysm had occurred there. The northern side, as far as the eyes could see, was a desolate landscape reminiscent of a carpet-bombing campaign, while the south slope revealed an ongoing reclaiming of the beauty and lushness that had once made that island one of the world's more coveted vacation destinations. As they began their descent, via the once enchanting stone-paved road now being encroached or reclaimed by nature, they observed the huge plane descending and then carefully being placed on the ground. It was in the middle of what was some time ago a large piazza around which houses and boutiques full of happy villagers and some of the vacationers retreated away from the lavishness and the incongruous western *viva la vida loca* atmosphere of the seaside hotels.

"Hey guys," Taggart said as he put his arms around Lance and Tina's shoulders, "Artie did a great job as a wedding planner, didn't he? Too bad I'm not licensed to perform a marriage, I would be glad to..."

"Oh Tag, would you..." Tina pleaded.

"I'm just saying... look at those magnificent hotels, that beach down there, the water... Lance, my man, you popped the question yet? Well, you had better hurry; I'm getting in the mood myself. In this setting, she might be able to convince me. I told you she's been after me forever."

"Shut up!" Tina protested, "You didn't really tell him that; did you?"

"We're best buds now, we confide... I told him you're not pretty enough for me. I cannot see why he thinks you're all that. I just can't see it."

"Ok, that's it; you're not invited."

"To what?"

"To the wedding."

"What, are you guys in trouble? All right, Lance! Way to go, you sneaky... only thing is her father's going to come after you, dude. Listen, South America can be a nice place to hide out and..."

"Alright... you can be best man if you keep quiet about it," Tina said; then addressing Lance, "Baby, you think the chief can marry us, we have to do it before I start showing. We don't want the pictures to say..."

"Wait a minute, are you serious?" Taggart frowned.

"I know, my darling," Lance answered, ignoring Taggart, "tell me if it sounds crazy, but I was thinking we go to Cronart... we could honeymoon there..."

"Oh... the honeymoon!" Tina slowly respired, "Anywhere, my love, as long as your golden bow caresses on my Stradivarius, I'll make beautiful music..."

"Golden bow? Now, wait a minute..." Taggart tried to interrupt.

"And as long as the sweet nectar of your tulip..."

"Excuse me, we're on a mission here," Taggart interrupted in an attempt at stopping Lance and Tina, who were at that moment sitting on a patch of grass holding hands, and leaning in for what was about to be the most passionate kiss since the last presidential inauguration.

"Did you hear something, Lance darling?" Tina asked.

"Only our hearts beating in perfect harmony, my queen," lance loudly whispered before both lovers became hysterical with laughter.

"Oh, very, very, very good," Taggart pouted.

"Aw... What's the matter, big bad Tag can't take a little show of tender loving lust?" Tina kidded.

"Sorry prof, couldn't help it; like you said, that's the power of love," Lance sang.

"Good one," Taggart said, "but I'm still telling her dad."

They were still laughing and joking when fifty yards from the bottom the sound of lightning followed immediately by that of a crash breached the tranquility. Looking in the direction of the noise, they had less than a second to see a balcony of the closest hotel crashing to the ground, and the figure of the man who had been on it following a strange curve into the sea.

"Did you see that?" Lance shouted, "I hope that was Artie's work... yes it was."

"That must have been Artie's diversionary tactic." Taggart assumed.

"But who was that?" Tina said.

"He intercepted a sniper who had his sight on the plane," Lance replied, "he wants us to be vigilant; there may be others."

"Look, Rotcod's coming out;" Taggart said, "there are two armed men... our two friends, A9 and B12."

"The noise must have spooked them; let's be very careful advancing," Tina advised.

"We'll approach through the main street. Should we have our hands up?" Lance asked.

"Yeah, good idea!" Taggart agreed.

They carefully circled toward the main street that connected the hotels to the village and stepped onto the brick roadway with hands raised. As they came into view, Rotcod became agitated and started to bark out orders,

"Stay in the middle of the street. Keep your hands where they can be seen! What in hell was that?"

"Listen," Lance yelled back, "there is another party lurking around. We don't know who they are, so let's do this and get out of here."

"Ok, but remember what I said, no tricks or..."

"We're wasting time, sir; can we tend to the business at hand?" Taggart suggested.

"Sure, where is it?"

"It's in the professor's bag," Lance said, "I'd like to go in and see the alien and then we can conclude this."

Rotcod agreed, but as Lance got to ten feet of him, he grabbed the gun from A9 and told Lance to,

"Stop right there! Tell the professor to bring the tablet to the agent, or else this will be your permanent resting place; and I'm not going to discuss this at any length whatsoever; you understand?"

"I understand, but I believe your bargaining chip is no more. Now, slowly turn around, sir."

Rotcod turned to see Spock standing at the plane door smiling and sporting the biggest and meanest looking assault riffle that anyone had ever seen. He addressed Rotcod with,

"My name is Pofila; in your world I would be Dr. Pofila, but you can continue to call me the alien. I like the status; it's a compliment. With few exceptions, including this brave agent who has just risked his life to rescue me from such a contemptible human such as you, Dr Rotcod, and this magnanimous group of young people, your race has a long way before you arrive where you so self-deceivingly think you are. Your pilot has been convinced to take a little nap; he will be all right. Drop your weapons; I would not want to show you my impersonation of a human..."

"Excuse me, American agents," a slightly accented voice from the other side of the plane suddenly shouted," you are surrounded and outnumbered; any more hostility toward anyone of us and we will be forced to strike back. We're coming out now; please put down your weapons and stay calm."

"Good!" Pofila exhaled as he lay down the gun, "I could not go through with it anyway."

A second later, the village became alive; there was movement everywhere. Men in full protective gear poured out of every store, window, and bush to surround the group in a tight circle. One of them stepped in and walked toward Lance, intently studied his face, and then finally said,

"So this is the great Lance, ha! We meet again. We have to pick a bone together. Perhaps I can start what you did not finish last time."

"Do we know each other?" Lance asked, "I don't know what you're trying to say, sir."

"I believe he has a bone to pick with you," Taggart explained, "and he wants to finish what you started... I speak a little chiglish."

"You Americans are immune to radiation?" the man asked.

"You Chinese are always so concerned for your wellbeing?" Lance shot back."

"Captain," the Chinese turned to the leader of the platoon, "the men can take off their masks."

He shed his protective suit and headgear; Lance looked into his eyes and at that moment realized,

"You must be the gifted psychic that I have been told about. Now, how can we help you?"

"Déjà vu, Lance! Look around, doesn't this all look familiar?" Tina whispered, "He was there in our dream; you fought him that... night."

Lance turned to face the man, but the Chinese had taken a martial art stance; he was ready for battle. He took several steps back and let out a scream. Still shrieking, he sprinted back toward Lance who was standing motionless, rigid, and slightly leaning forward. His palms were facing forward at hips level; eyes and face empty of any expression. His attacker was a fraction of a second from making contact when Lance's hand materialized in front of the targeted spot on his body. That was repeated time and time again. Wherever the Chinese' foot, or hand, or knee, or elbow appeared, it was met with an almost omnipresent and unmovable obstacle. He realized after five minutes of total and desperate aggression that he was overmatched. He fell to the ground exhausted, and yelled out an order in Chinese. His comrades raised and cocked their weapons.

"Enough! We want the artifact right now," the captain impatiently demanded, "we would rather have it with nobody getting hurt but..."

"Okay captain, it's just a matter of protocol," Lance said, "Would you please allow us a moment to come to a consensus?"

"Five seconds," the captain agreed.

Lance called for everyone to huddle. The four of them assembled in a tight circle; they appeared to be engaged in a serious discussion. At the five seconds mark, Lance strolled over to Rotcod and handed him the replica of the artifact that Artie had generated.

"I keep my promises," Lance told him, and then addressing the captain, "It's his decision; he's in charge here."

He walked back to the group, which then was immediately snapped up by a rod of light. A stream of bullets went pointlessly up toward the heavens.

The Media

"He is a nice man, isn't he," Tina said.

"He is; that's why I voted for him," Taggart agreed, "Finally the public will be told the truth about ET's."

"Well... I wouldn't hold my hopes up too high," Spock cautioned, "When it comes to the subject of space aliens, there's a kind of ingrained paranoia about public awareness. I am sure that it is being communicated to him as we speak."

"What about his promise to get Phil out," Taggart asked, "He can do that, can he not?"

"Don't worry," the chief replied, "I received his personal assurance on it; your friend is probably on his way over here as we speak."

"Put the volume up," Lance requested, "I think they've just announced the Defense Secretary."

On the television screen, the Defense Secretary of the United States was displaying the grave look of a government official about to inform the country of a declaration of war. Everyone in the room straightened up and leaned toward the set, waiting perhaps for that proud moment when the incredible story that they had just lived is told; and who knows, they might get some recognition!

Once the alien, inside his human host, had returned to his ship in the belly of the mountain, and Spock been rayed back up to the craft, Artie brought them back to Washington DC to help inform the occupants of the blockading alien ship of Pofila's release and whereabouts. They were able to communicate to the White House that they were the human rescuers, and that they wished to zip down for a visit with the president. Access was granted. Following a most unusual, frenzied, though convivial meeting with the charming and grateful leader, they were led to a comfortable lounge. They were going to be debriefed by the NSA and others as soon as some high level meeting had taken place. Everyone was in celebratory mood until the announcement by the Secretary that the nation's capital had been the subject of a test, the aim of which was to ensure that it could be sealed off in the event of an attack.

A long, painful, and almost mournful "Oh" emptied out all lungs. Everyone slumped back in his or her chair; hope had died again! No one wanted to validate with words the feeling that a last chance at salvation had been missed, and that the truth, which might have set humankind free from its arrogance, had been enchained once again. They had an urgent message from Pofila to deliver publicly to the Congress; a revelation by the president that a superior alien race had just visited us would have authenticated it. How will they deal with the danger that is literally raining down on human civilization? How will they make these leaders extricate their collective head from the sand and protect the people who at the very moment were being used as living Petri dishes? Earth's inhabitants were inhaling and absorbing through their skins sperm-like filaments almost invisible to the naked eye; they were being seeded, fertilized, and harvested. Some in the government, like Dr. Rotcod, with hope of prominent ranks in the new order to come, were perhaps unwittingly complicitous.

They listened distractedly to the obligatory and redundant comments, interpretation, and clarification of the usual experts, until an image on the screen drew Tina's attention.

"Lance, isn't that your friend?"

"It is Chris; what is he saying?" Lance asked, looking at the man on the screen about to be interviewed.

"... and it has been the subject of conjectures of all kinds. Conspiracy theorists have been busy suggesting one scheme after another. Kyle, we have here a young man who claims to have a different take on the happenings in Washington. His reason for speaking out is to save his friend from what he claims to be a secret government agency bent on suppressing by any means the truth about alien technology. I'll let him explain himself. Go ahead Chris."

"My friend came by my place early this morning. He was looking for a place to hide from government agents. They found out that he was in possession of alien technology..."

"How did your friend come by this... er, alien technology?"

"Well, they were on the run. The agents had followed them to my place; they had to leave before I got all the details, but I was supposed to hear from them hours ago. I think they're being held somewhere; tortured maybe. I want the public to know that the government is holding Lance Avignon and his professors illegally. His father needs to know that his son is missing."

"His college professors?"

"Yes."

"You are saying his college professors are involved as well?

"They're on the run together..."

"And this has what to do with the quarantine of Washington D.C.?"

"It was no quarantine. I don't think it's just coincidence that it's all happening at the same time. He told me that he had something that any government on earth would like to possess. The aliens don't want us to have it either; I guess they came back for it. They found out somehow

that lance was taken to Washington, so they put a siege on the place until they get their stuff back."

"That's a very interesting assumption," the reporter smiled, "but you look like a smart young man; don't you think that..."

"Don't patronize me, sir," Chris rejoined, "Listen, why do you think the government waited until now to give an explanation? Why wasn't the president evacuated first with his family? They must have given the thing back to the aliens; think about it. Oh, you're the Media, you don't think; you just report... I mean repeat, don't you. I guess all those people in Jersey were suffering from mass hallucination this morning, just like your silly expert said."

"Well, as I said, very interesting... back to you, Kyle."

"God! In all the excitement, I forgot that I told him we'd come back for him," Lance sighed.

"I guess he was worried about you, Lance," Tina said.

"And he put himself directly in the line of fire; that's the selfless act of a real friend," Taggart added.

"Yep, he's real," Lance said, "He was a little disappointed that I left when I did; that's all."

"I have to leave now," the chief announced as he stood up, "I have to be back on the job, but it was good getting out, especially with you guys. That was quite an experience; it was kind of fun I must say. They need to have a formal briefing with you; I am sure that some covert congressional committee will have plenty for me. They know where to find me. Agent Novitz will stay with you until it's over. It will not be so bad; they owe you, we all owe you. And... stop by headquarters anytime; be good to see you again."

Everyone stood up to thank and greet him goodbye. He received a hug from Lance and a kiss from Tina. Taggart approached and with a sober look said,

"Sir, it has been a great privilege to make your acquaintance, and it would be an honor if you would allow me to spy under you; well, not under you, that would be uncomfortable... I mean under your stewardship, sir. I wanna be like Spock!"

"Okay, I tell you what, if agent... Spock is willing to help you be like him, I'll let you spy, but in a land far, far away from me... or the free world for that matter," the chief giggled.

As he turned to leave the room, professor Rhoades appeared at the door, with Roseanne clutching his left bicep as if she would never let go of him; as she did with the artifact case earlier. All rose as one to welcome him back and possibly check him for signs of torture... or hickeys.

"Was it worth it?" Taggart whispered to him, "I bet it was, you..."

"Professor Rhoades, Roseanne," the chief greeted them.

"Mr. Westbrook... er, Mr. Director..." Roseanne replied as she hurriedly pealed off Phil's arm and nearly stood at attention.

"Who was that?" Phil inquired.

"That was CIA director Len Westbrook," Roseanne whispered.

"Westbrook?" everybody sounded loudly.

"Is everybody thinking what I'm thinking? Why didn't it ring a bell before? Could it..." Tina wondered.

"Yes, that's why all of that was allowed to happen," Taggart surmised, "he's the Queen's husband."

"Oh... that hypocrite!" Lance fumed, "He's acting like he's the victim; like, oh I was duped..."

"Well, he probably didn't have the true facts; he was as much in the dark as we..."

"Oh, come on, Phil, he had his own man... and woman working on the inside," Taggart differed.

All eyes turned in Spock's direction; he smiled, shook his head, and then asked,

"Oh, is this the part of the movie where they try to figure out who the mole is? You know Tag, if this is the way you begin your career as a spy, it's a crushing disappointment. Lance, your friend was right about coincidence; but in this case, it is. They just happened to be husband

and wife, and I can confidently say that you were not the reason why they married twenty-five years ago. I'll tell you what else you may consider though, three of the youngest and most intelligent kids ever to be admitted in Mensa being born in the same town; blocks from one another. Oh, that's not all; there are many such... coincidences. Guess when I gained this gift of ESP... on March 14, 1991. Guess who was born on that day... that's right, Lance Avignon. Wait, I'm not done; what else do all four of you have in common? Here it is; a single parent, whose partner... poof, vanished, disappeared, raised each of the four of you, and not one of those remaining parents ever remarried. Why did the aforementioned Mr. Avignon decide out of the blue to enroll at the very university where the three musketeers would be in need of a fourth with his talents; a dream perhaps? Why did the beautiful Miss King decide at last to unbind her own psychic abilities, which she had suppressed so stubbornly in the past? Oh, one more, oh please one more; why did the good professor Schaffhausen leave such a tightly knit group to become an archeologist who would go on to unearth arguably the most significant artifact ever? A CIA plot you say... No? Coincidence... maybe? Serendipity... nothing? Oh, too bad... such a smart group!"

"I see what you mean," Taggart retreated, "ok... er, perhaps some mad Hollywood casting director..."

"What do you think Roseanne?" Tina asked, "I notice you haven't said much. You must have a perspective on all this."

"I am strictly a personnel administrator and a research scientist. When it comes to specific cases, if I do not need to know, I don't; I understood and accepted it. My father was an agent, and when he died, I was adopted by my uncle; I'm accustomed to the protocol." Roseanne replied, "But what professor Taggart just said in jest reminds me of something you said, Phil. When the three of you were still children, some guy came to your town to interview you and your parents, and then he went on TV to declare that you were alien hybrids..."

"Yeah, I remember," Tina reflected, "our parents were furious."

"And they forbade speaking to anyone after that," Taggart recalled.

"Oh God, they were absolutely fanatical in their loathing of the media," Phil added.

"But you know, I did not mind too much being an alien hybrid, in fact I think I enjoyed it," Tina shared.

"Heck, that was way better than freak, nerd, or geek; I didn't like indigo child either" Phil smiled.

"Hey dude, I was proud," Taggart boomed, "I felt downright superior; I became a star child, a space cadet, a sky walker. I was connected, man! It made missing having a dad easier."

"Hear, hear!" Phil agreed.

"Well, if it wasn't true, and those situations did not concur by happenstance, how do you explain all of it?" Roseanne asked.

Again, all attention was directed at Spock. He slowly stood, took a long look at the group and,

"When I began investigating this case, I was not sure what the outcome would be. I was mystified immediately by the lack of anything suspicious in professor Taggart's conduct or affiliations, hard to believe, right? I was determined, however, to find a common thread. I did a background on everyone that was exposed to you, professor. In my line of work, I'm accustomed to the strange and unusual, but I had never encountered anything like it. I was faced with so many abnormalities that I started to question my objectivity; I thought I was getting too fixated. There were changes in my own behavior that others and I were beginning to question.

As we now know, I was working on an agenda not my own. Lance perhaps can appreciate this, that although we are no more guided by a foreign element, our mental abilities are permanently altered; I'll even say amplified. That second time around with Pofila, I was able to explore him as he did me. Oh by the way, that memory editing did not work; he was still able to read me because he went deeper that the mental. I could tell that his initial intention had been to have me steal the artifact and bring it to his ship, but he had a secondary mission, which was to study us and assess the possibility of peaceful co-habitation of earth. Perhaps he was starting to be protective of us, or of earth, his prospective future home, and he decided to hang around to solve the enigma. I was expecting to find him to be the mastermind behind the strange occurrences, but he was just as intrigued. I think...well, I believe that he was as much a pawn as we all were."

"So then... hum, who was the Chessmaster? Roseanne queried.

"What about those guys who were chasing us?" Tina proposed.

"I don't know," Lance doubted, "judging by the way things played out, I don't think they had it in them. But I do think they were at least the agents of the evil against which we were apparently being prepared to protect. I have a strong suspicion that they were two-timing Mr. Rotcod by working with the Chinese as well. By the way, Artie assured me that I will know what to do if and when they come back and want to cause trouble."

"You know Artie wanted to stay here with you, but you were the nanny or the big brother; daddy had come home, so the choice was simple," Spock reasoned, "We should not have been able to access the artifact the way we did; Pofila was quite puzzled by it. Professor Rhoades' invention was one of those fortuitous and timely concurrences."

"Tell me, agent Spock, why do you think you were able to probe him so easily this time around," Phil asked.

"I have been mulling it over, and my enhanced intuitive sense tells me that he allowed me to, but he manipulated my consciousness and decided what and how much I could glimpse. I also think that he has great psychic powers, even by his people's standards. But I still believe there is a higher power at work; the ultimate Grandmaster if you will."

"You mean..." Tina looked up.

"Really... the big guy himself?" Taggart queried.

"Come on, people, let's not get messiahnistic," Phil cautioned, "I'm still adjusting to my new belief in space aliens and all that."

"Is it just me, or are there a lot of similarities between what's been happening and exactly that premise?" Lance wondered.

"What premise?" Phil asked

"I see what he means," Tina interjected, "The Messiah came down to earth, he left the word, he promised to return to vanquish Satan, raise the chosen few, establish a new world order, and reestablish the kingdom of his father; read the bible!"

"Is that what you meant, Lance?" Taggart smiled.

"Yes, exactly!"

"Oh! That's cute! You two are going to start ending each other's sentences as well? Ok, Roseanne... quick, what is Phil thinking?"

"Shut up!" Tina blushed, "Jealous... I saw you checking out that pretty intern. She's a good candidate for you; why didn't you... I'm sure she was reading your mind."

"I was reading his mind!" Phil said, "I can tell you, it wasn't very spiritual."

"So... hum, where is my uncle?" Roseanne interrupted.

"Oh, we're sorry; you don't know, do you?" Spock answered, "He was taken by the Chinese, but they're in the process of returning him. I'm sure you'll see him soon."

"By the way, thank you, agent Novitz," Roseanne said while snuggling even more tightly against Phil, " he told me that something you said made him see the light."

"Oh, er... you're welcome; but the light is so beautifully bright; he was bound to... grab it. Sorry, I'm not much of a poet."

"Yes, not really," Phil laughingly agreed.

The clinking sound heard outside the room reminded them that they had not had anything to eat in a while. A young woman walked in pushing a rolling silver tray; she transferred some of the scrumptious goodies to the coffee table, and introduced herself with,

"Good morning again, ladies and gentlemen, my name is Keyla Mancini and I am an intern here on the president's staff. The first Lady thought you might need some sustenance after your long ordeal. The meeting should be over shortly. In the meantime, enjoy! Is there anything else I can get you?"

Everybody was all smiles as they thanked her profusely. She turned to leave but,

"There is one thing," Tina stopped her, "My brother Taggart here is usually quite gregarious; he is a little shy right now, but he thinks that you are very attractive. You made quite an impression on him; he just shared with me that he would love to have dinner with you sometime..."

"Thank you, Taggart, I am flattered," she smiled.

She reached into her blazer's breast pocket for a card, which she slipped in his hand with a handshake while she mouthed, *"call me."*

He followed her sinuous curves out of the room, waited the residual light imprint in his eyes to recede snugly into his memory, and then,

"I am going to kill you," he playfully threatened Tina, "Nah... thank you, baby; mwah! I love you. Wow... she is cute!"

"Look how excited he is. I've never seen him so thrilled about meeting someone." Phil laughed.

"This means she likes me, right? Taggart exhaled.

"Does she like you?" Spock replied, "She locked in on you the moment she walked in. I bet you she volunteered for this. You think she always carries one card in her breast pocket?"

"Really?"

As everyone swiftly descended on the delicacies, laughter reverberated inside the room. Taggart was delightfully mocked, teased, tickled, poked, head-rubbed, and showered with chants of *"Tag and Keyla sitting in a tree k-i-s-s-i-n-g."*

"Wow, baby," Lance addressed Tina, "our island is going to be crowded; do we have to share?"

"Only if Tag promises to behave."

"I think he will; she looks like she can convince him to."

"Yeah... in more ways than one."

"I think you're right, Miss King"

"Excuse me, Mr. Avignon, it's baby for you."

"Oh, baby!"
Laughter!
Googly eyes!
Kiss...
Er... huh hum!
"I love you!"
"I love you more!"
Awwww...

Outline

- Lance is a bright and gifted student at a New York state University. He is asked to be a subject in a dream research project headed by professor Rhoades who has been told of his talents by Miss King, the English instructor with whom Lance has madly fallen in love.
- A friend of both Rhoades and King, professor Taggart, having learned of Lance's gift for 'seeing' in dreams, gets in the act in order to have old texts he found in the Middle East, near Jerusalem, deciphered.
- 10,000 years ago (earth time,) facing persecution and seeing the writing on the wall, alien scientists searched the heavens for a suitable planet where all knowledge could be safely stored until better times.
- A new invention, later called 'the Travel Light,' allowed an object to be transported across vast interstellar distances at speed exponentially faster than the speed of light.
- A minority of that society did not believe in the good of science, which was blamed for all the ills of that period.
- Religious right-wing zealots took over millenniums ago and forbade anything to do with scientific research and the paranormal.
- Rebels pursued research underground, they discovered old museum of scientific discoveries. One young man in particular started to experiment with found prototypes left over from the

free days. His research uncovered that matter was the last step in the evolution of E = Mc2; light having been the first.

- Rich, influential man helps rebels' cause but has his own agenda. He went to earth to retrieve old texts; merged with CIA agent (nicknamed Spock.)
- Chinese agents kidnapped Miss. Tina King in order to force the group's cooperation.
- Shadowy government organization, OSID (Outer Space invaders Defense,) created to safeguard earth against alien invasions, helps rescue Tina; and soon after, the organization's interest in the artifact becomes apparent.
- Alien ship arrives on earth to rescue ET, who has been captured by OSID. They isolate wash DC by surrounding it with an invisible impenetrable dome.
- Lance & co. pursue Rotcod who is on his way to the Sinai Mountain to find his prisoner's alien craft.
- A battle ensues between the heroes' craft and alien associates of Rodcod's. A strategy of 'time and seek' is used by Artie to evade and lose them in other dimensions.
- An island in the Mediterranean is the setting for a confrontation with Chinese agents, intent on seizing the artifact.